A twist in fate

BY

JENNIE LYNN PETERS

Honey Blossom Publishing

Library of Congress Control Number: 2019916636

Copyright 2018 by Jennie Peters

ISBN 978-1-7341613-0-4 (paperback)

978-1-7341613-1-1 (ebook)

978-1-7341613-2-8 (hardcover)

Author photograph by Sarah Peters

1

A big thank you to everyone who helped me along this journey. Without your love and support through babysitting, reading my book, and most importantly cheering me on, I would never have brought my story to the world. I love you all.

Pronunciation guide available in back of book

1

"Mrs. Takara?"

"Yes Sarah?" She says before sipping on her steaming green tea.

"Tell me another story, one about Nihon." I pick up my teacup with the swirls of clouds etched in black ink on the side.

She chuckles, "I'm glad you asked, I've been meaning to tell you an important story, one about the princess."

I involuntarily scooch to the edge of my seat, clutching the warm teacup in my hands.

"There's a world far from here, the lands rich and the air clear, the people carry the traditions of ancient Japan." She slurps more tea before continuing.

"Such a place would seem peaceful, but as you know, the yokai threaten the very existence of mankind. A princess, blessed with extraordinary powers is destined to destroy the demons and save Nihon."

"I know that part, tell me something new."

"To defeat the yokai she will join forces with her true love."

"True love conquers all." I snicker. "That's so corny."

Cocking an eyebrow she replies, "Is that so? Perhaps that's enough for today." She leans on the arm of her red floral sofa.

"No, please go on." I'm perched on the very edge of the seat.

"So eager, you'll get your chance soon enough."

"What is that supposed to mean?" To fall in love?

"Relax child, sit back and drink your tea."

I reluctantly sink to the back of my chair. The old clock hanging on the wall begins to chime.

"Oh my, it's nine o'clock already. Dear you'd better head on home before your mother calls."

I set down my ceramic cup on the cherry wood coffee table. We both know neither of my parents will phone.

"Thanks so much for sweeping my floors. Your help is always appreciated." She attempts to hand me ten dollars.

"No, your stories are all the payment I need."

"Take, it. You need to have play money for this summer."

Hesitantly I accept the gift and shove it in the stiff front pockets of my jeans. She's right, Mom and Dad won't be jumping to give me an allowance for activities.

"Bye Mrs. Takara, I'll see you in a few days to mow the lawn."

"I look forward to it." She holds the door open and waves to me.

I grab my bag and dash next door to my house. I quietly turn the knob, being careful to shut the door slowly and gradually release the knob. Even with my great efforts my mother notices.

"Back so soon?" She peers over the soft cover of her novel.

"Yes, I'm going to get ready for bed now."

"Don't stay up too late." She's back to reading before she finishes her sentence.

The house is eerily silent. Most days shouting fills the air. Going to Mrs. Takara's is a haven from the insanity here. Usually by this hour Dad is off with his girlfriend, and it's safe to come back.

I slump onto my bed and kick my shoes off. Nihon, how amazing it would be to live there. Adventure, culture– not living here. I snuggle up to my down feather pillow with the plaid print. I bet people have a life filled with purpose there, waging the battle against the half-human half-animal creatures trying to take over. If only a place like that really existed. Mrs. Takara has lots of stories about far off lands, Nihon being only one of them, but by far my favorite.

My parents think she's crazy, but they allow me to visit because she's the only other Asian nearby and my mom thinks it's good to learn about my heritage. Though she's Japanese, and Mom and I are Chinese. I guess Mom's desperate to drown out Dad's contribution to the gene pool.

2

"Come on Sarah! We'll be late for school," Missy shouts from downstairs.

"Coming!" I exclaim, grabbing my backpack.

"Let's go!" Missy's voice escalates with her increasing irritation.

I descend the white carpet stairs to please my ever impatient friend. "Bye Mom." I call out, but as usual she's too wrapped up in her romance novels to notice. I catch a whiff of her overpowering citrus perfume as I race by.

"Bye Mrs. Johnson," Missy says hurriedly as we rush out the door. "You make us late almost every day, you'd better help me clean my locker during lunch," Missy complains under her breath, but I'm undaunted by her remark. We dash down the street, racing against the traffic lights.

"I'm sorry, it's not like I try to. It's hard to sleep when I'm stressing about my parents." We stop briefly to wait at a stop light.

Her voice slows. "Oh, weren't they going to counseling or something?" Missy glances away guiltily.

"Not anymore, it's not like it was helping anyway. My mom caught my dad cheating with some woman he met online, on their anniversary of all things. After all these years, he's giving up on his family; it's as if he doesn't love us anymore," my voice quivers. I pause for a moment to regain my composure. "Things are falling apart." My attempts to hide my emotions are in vain as tears begin to stream down my cheeks. "Nothing I try works. I'm slowly fading into the background, becoming invisible in my own home."

Missy wraps her arms around me in a reassuring hug. "I will always be here for you Sarah. Your parents need to have their time right now to figure things out. It sucks, and you don't deserve this, but you'll make it through. You're stronger than you think."

The light changes, and we hurry across the busy street. Finally, we reach school and run to our class, sitting down with only seconds to spare before the bell rings.

Mrs. O'Brien begins her lecture, but the monotonous words fade out quickly. I sniffle and wipe my wet eyes.

"Psst, are you okay Sarah?" Brandon leans over and whispers.

My heart skips a beat in disbelief. *Is Brandon actually talking to me?* I've always had a thing for Brandon, but he's never really taken much interest in me.

8

I'm not too surprised, it's not like anyone else has either. My brown hair, brown eyes, and freckles aren't exactly the makings of someone worthwhile.

The screeching of the chalkboard comes to a halt. Mrs. O'Brien's kinky red curls bounce as she turns around. "Well, Brandon, do you have something you would like to share with the class?"

"No, Mrs. O'Brien." Brandon sits straight up, back stiff. Giggles spread across the classroom. Satisfied, she continues with the lesson.

Cautiously I move toward Brandon's desk, and carefully whisper, "Sorry about that, I'm fine."

I sink back into my desk, cringing with embarrassment.

The day drones on, until the teacher finally excuses us for lunch, and I rush to the school office. There Tammy, the receptionist, sits slumped at her desk, eating a ham sandwich. She awakens from her trance of boredom when I walk through the door.

"I know what you're here for. It came just in time before summer break." She puts down her sandwich to reach into her desk drawer. "The postman dropped this off only a few minutes ago." She pulls out a white envelope and hands it to me.

I hold the envelope in my hands, gazing at it as if it's the crystal ball about to predict my future. I've been waiting for weeks, and at last it's here.

"Don't just stand there and stare at it all day, open it." Her eyes are impatient and gleaming with excitement.

"But what if I didn't make the cut?"

"You'll never find out with that attitude. Open it!"

I tear open the seal and pull out the letter.

"What does it say?" She persists, leaning over the desk trying to catch a peak.

"Dear Ms. Johnson, we are pleased to inform you that you have been accepted into the summer psychology program at Willamette University."

Tammy sprints out of her seat. "That's great!" She races around her desk to give me a hug. "You are the only high schooler I know who would want to spend her summer studying, but I'm so happy for you. Have fun this summer."

"I will." For the first time today the stress of family life fades away. Things are finally looking up.

I resist telling my friends the big news, I want to tell Mom and Dad first. If I'm a good enough daughter, maybe they will have less to worry about, and get along with each other better. The rest of the day flies by, until I'm finally at home.

"Mom, Dad." I turn the large brass doorknob and burst inside our home, but I'm too late. They've already started yelling. Their declarations of anger ring throughout the house, bouncing off the fine china and mahogany wood floors. What is Dad doing home so early? Clinging tightly to my backpack I approach the scene.

"Shut up!" Mom yells. Dishes slam into the sink, and suds fly into the air.

"Why don't you take some of your own advice?" my father shouts back.

I cautiously interrupt the chaos, "Mom, Dad." They both turn to glare at me as if I'm the one they're fighting with. "I got into the study school I wanted, you know, the one for the university I will attend when I graduate. I got the acceptance letter today."

"Great, honey. Why don't you go to your room now?" Mom mutters. She brushes me off, just like every other day. We haven't had a real conversation since finger painting and hide-and-seek were our pastimes.

I drag my feet out of the room, trying to numb myself so I don't have to feel the sting of disappointment. Seconds later, I snap back to reality at the sound of Mom's fist slamming against the black granite counter-top. "You never listen to me. Why can't you ever be quiet and listen to me for once?" She yells these words at Dad, but hardly practices what she preaches.

I clench my backpack tighter and escape up the stairs. They should both shut up! Reaching my room I slam the door behind me. Slowly I slide down my bedroom door; tears stream down my face before I reach the floor. Still hearing their snide remarks, I climb into bed and reach for my feather pillow. I smother my face, hoping it will stifle the rumbling rampage from my parents below. It's useless.

No "congratulations" or "good job Sarah, we're so proud of you." For once I wish they would say something like that.

"I'm leaving!" Dad's voice booms through the entire house.

"Fine! Walk out like you always do," Mom shouts back.

The door slams, and the whole house falls silent. The only sound is the fading footsteps of Dad leaving. Out of the emptiness, sobs and sniffles from Mom rise up the stairs.

I'm afraid I have no choice but to go downstairs and console her.

There she is, sitting on the dirty floor, picking up the pieces of chopped chicken and broccoli that was to be dinner. I kneel down next to her. While clasping my arms around my mother, I gently murmur, "Mom, I love you."

She looks up at me, the dark circles around her eyes reveal the constant stress she's been under. "I love you too, sweetie. That's why I need to tell you something." Mom wipes away the mascara streaks on her cheeks. "Dad and I are getting a divorce."

My heart stops. "Divorce?" Chills run down my spine. Ever since the fighting became more constant, I feared them getting a divorce. I thought I had prepared myself, but part of me could never accept that it would really happen.

"Sarah, I'm sending you to live with Grandma and Grandpa. I can't give you the attention you deserve right now."

My chest tightens and I can hardly breathe, like someone's punched me in the gut. "What? But Mom, what about my friends? My summer school? Mrs. Takara?" My eyes burn and swell from the crying.

"It's already been settled. You'll leave tomorrow."

"But..." I stammer.

"Don't start with me Sarah. I've had enough tonight."

"You don't care about me!" I jerk away.

"You know that's not true."

I stop listening and run out of the kitchen and up the stairs, I trip on the last step because my vision is so blurred. Slamming my door and rushing to my bed, I can't help but to want to scream. "Ah!" Why, why, *why?* Why me? I wish my family was like everyone else's, normal!

I can't stay here any longer, I rush to the window and thrust it open. I step onto the rooftop for the first floor. I pause briefly, where will I go? I look across the yard to see Mrs. Takara's lights still on. I close the window behind me and shimmy along the side of the house until I reach the tall oak tree on the south-east corner of the house. I firmly grasp the branch just beyond the roof and swing down. The pull of gravity is more than I had expected, my fingertips slip off the papery bark and I stumble on the moist lawn.

My elbow is sore, but otherwise I'm unscathed. Again I glance upward to the beacon of the neighbor's house. I stand up and brush off the dirt and blades of grass clinging to my skin. I sneak to the front room window. Mom is on the tan sofa, engrossed in her book, bits of broccoli stuck to her black hair. I turn and run away.

I find myself rapping on the red door of Mrs. Takara's. There's no answer. I try again, a little louder this time, and finally the deadbolt slides back.

Her gray hair, which is normally in a tight bun, has been let down in waves over her shoulders. "Come in dear, what are you doing out at this hour?"

I open my mouth to reply, but the hard lump prevents more than a squeak from passing through.

"Tea will sooth that throat of yours." She says while placing her arm around me and guiding me through the doorway.

I sit down on the couch and place my sweaty palms over my face, not sure what I'm doing here.

Mrs. Takara brings a steaming pot of tea and places it on the bamboo print pot holder resting on the table. She pours a cup for each of us. After I take my first sip she says, "Now, tell me everything."

I recount the unsettling evening that just occurred, all the while a frim grimace rests on her face. When I finish she clinks her teacup on the table. "What if I told you there's a way for you to escape this situation?"

"Like, come to live with you?"

"Yes, in a way."

"That would be wonderful." I slide to the edge of my seat, sloshing my tea. "Sorry."

"Don't worry about that dear. Follow me." She leads me to a back room, one she uses for Christmas decorations and other storage. Stretching to the top shelf of the built in cupboard, she pulls down a package wrapped with a burlap sack and twine. "You'll need a change of clothes, those are filthy. This is all I have. You can dress in the spare bedroom."

I nod and proceed to the guest room slash sewing room. I pull on the end of the ribbon, the string unravels and the cloth unfolds. A perfectly pressed yellow kimono with a red ribbon is revealed. It takes several tries to figure out how to properly tie the obi and secure the outfit. I return to Mrs. Takara and twirl.

"Lovely, these will match the outfit." She passes me a pair of wooden and leather sandals.

"Thanks!" I remove my sweet soaked socks and slip the sandals on.

"There is something else I would like to show you." We walk back to the storage room. Knocking over a box of Halloween decorations, she retrieves a scrap of paper. Covering the black ink symbol with her hand, she mutters under her breath.

"Is everything okay Mrs. Takara?"

Ignoring me, white light bursts from beneath her palm. A dark mist surrounds us.

"Um, Mrs. Takara."

"This is your way out, all you have to do is touch the symbol. You're new name is Rika, I will join you when the portal recharges."

"What?"

"If you're going to go you must do it now before it loses power, otherwise you'll have to wait a few days and considering what happened tonight with your parents that won't be an option."

I gulp and nod, before stretching forth my hand. Immediately I'm weightless and Mrs. Takara has vanished. I float along with no destination in sight, the room completely gone.

My heart beats fast as panic sets in. What have I done? My parental problems will have to take a backseat.

A bright light flashes as before, I'm standing in a fully bloomed cherry orchard. Where am I?

3

My knees buckle and I collapse to the ground, hard packed dirt greets my knees, scraping them both. This can't be happening. The cherry trees surrounding me release delicate pink petals that float down. I have no idea where I am, I don't suppose clicking my heels three times will help at all?

The sun is setting, casting a bright orange hue on the cherry trees. Where am I supposed to go? The air grows colder with each passing minute, a shiver runs through me. Seeking shelter is my top priority now. Perhaps civilization's beyond this orchard. I begin marching along the rows of cherry trees, with no real destination in sight. I walk and walk, disregarding my aching feet and the blisters forming under the straps of my sandals. The sun completely disappears beyond the horizon, the sky rapidly darkens.

Stars pop out one by one, and the night is unusually bright. Up in the sky there is not one moon, but three. My chest tightens. *Where am I?* The trees are endless. After all this time there's no sign I've made any progress.

Frustrated I lean against the rough trunk of a cherry tree. "None of this was supposed to happen!" I shout to the three moons. "I should have gone to summer school, Mom and Dad should have stayed together, I shouldn't be on this alien planet!" My fingers clench into a fist, and without thinking it through, I slam my fist into the jagged bark of the tree.

Pain sears through my hand, my fingers pulsate, and blood drips down. I grasp my wounded hand and squeeze it tight. Another stupid move made by yours truly. Twigs snap behind me.

"Mrs. Takara? Is that you?" I shove away from the tree and run toward the sound, a field is visible through a patch of branches. I race forward, ignoring my injured hand, when someone blocks my path. His body and face are human, but the huge black wings on his back, large yellow bird feet, and jet-black hair resembles a crow. I stop dead in my tracks, pulse racing. He's at least seven or eight feet high, and quite handsome to my surprise.

My first instinct is to run away, but a sudden calmness washes over me. He comes toward me with a plastered on grin, lifting my chin with his calloused hand.

Leaning in, he whispers in my ear, "I witnessed your temper tantrum. Alien planet? I don't suppose you're the long lost princess?"

This guy's delusional if he thinks I'm some sci-fi princess. I have to get away, but my legs won't move. There's a sensation of trust, and my head feels fuzzy. He kisses my forehead and takes my hand. "Come with me. I've been waiting years to kill you."

I try with all my might to clear my head. This is a mutant creature, trying to kill me! I shouldn't be letting him get near me, let alone kiss me. For a split second I break free from the trance and shove him away. A flash of red light shoots from my hands, violently throwing him back. "Whoa." I stare down at my hands with amazement.

"You just had to make this difficult." His face hardens to a scowl as he spreads his wings out and charges toward me with determination in his eyes. I turn to escape, but he grabs me around the waist and takes flight. He quickly soars upward over the cherry orchard.

"No!" I scream, pounding on his chest with all my might. "No, no, no!" I continue to slam my fists against his hard muscles; with my next blow, the red light returns and shines brightly with every punch. To my relief, he can't stand the beating for long. With a groan of pain, he releases me and flies away. I quickly plummet down toward the ground. I close my eyes tight, waiting to hit the hard soil of the orchard, but instead strong arms grab me. I open my eyes expecting to see the bird creature, but it's someone else. I've got to get away, there's no telling what he wants of me.

While devising an escape plan, I glance upward and notice he's looking down at me with a puzzled expression. He's not trying to kill me yet, that's a good sign. We stare at each other for a moment, and I'm transfixed by his golden cat-like eyes. His face is young, yet chiseled and defined. His square jaw enhances his masculine perfection.

"I saw what you did to that bird demon." He speaks to me in a deep, growling voice.

"I can do that to you too if you don't put me down right now." I squirm, trying to get out of his arms.

19

Laughing he smiles down at me. "Whoa there, if you don't want to be held, you could just say so." His voice is lighter and less intimidating now. Gently, he sets me down on my feet and continues to hold onto my arm until I gain my footing. "You could be a little nicer; I did save your life after all."

"I'm sorry, I thought you were one of those monsters." My tense shoulders relax and I let out a sigh of relief.

He releases my arm, and as his hand drops it reveals a lion's tail swinging back and forth behind him. I spoke too soon. He is shorter than the crow, but still close to seven feet tall. I back away, he has lion ears too, how did I not notice that?

"Don't worry," he reassures, "I won't hurt you. I am yokai, but I'm not like those demons. I try my best to aid humans, instead of hunting them down to feast on their soul." He clears his throat. "I'm the protector of Unmei, a village just outside this orchard. When I saw that bird yokai flying overhead, I came to investigate, and lucky for you I did."

"Thank you."

"You're not from around here, are you? Most people know better than to wander the orchard at night. Unfortunately it is an excellent place for predators to hide."

"Actually, I'm a long way from home."

"Then, you can stay with me tonight."

A shirtless, handsome, ripped man with six pack abs, wearing only a loin cloth made from lion furs wants me to spend the night with him.

"Excuse me?" I squeak. He's hot but I'm not that kind of girl.

"Um, that came out all wrong. I meant you can stay with me and my little sister, if you'd like."

I try to hide my face behind my hair, embarrassed at the misunderstanding. "Oh, alright then." It's not like I can remain here all night, who knows what else is lurking in the shadows.

He leads the way out of the cherry orchard and we stroll straight into what could be ancient Japan. Dirt roads, small hut houses; it's like the documentary I watched in school back in the eighth grade.

This can't be real, can it? Lanterns line the outsides of wooden buildings, illuminating the main pathway through town. Exotic spices waft through the air, causing my nose to tingle. Human villagers stroll past us, all keeping a respectful distance. They are Japanese in appearance, from their long black hair wrapped up into a thick bun atop their heads, to the simple kimonos of varying colors they wear.

As we continue down the path the buildings become farther and farther apart, until no more are left in sight, only a dim light up ahead. As we get closer I can see the small hut it illuminates. A human girl, about eight years old, comes running out, leaping onto the lion with a hug.

"Brother, you're home. Where in Nihon have you been?" The child is latched on tight, clinging to his bare arms.

Nihon, I'm on Nihon. Those stories Mrs. Takara told me growing up, they're true! I draw in a deep breath to steady my nerves. Yokai, ancient Japan, powers, it's all making sense now.

After a few moments, she realizes that I'm standing behind him. Letting go, she points at me. "Who is she?"

He turns to face me. "Hm, I'm not sure. I never asked her name."

"What? You brought some girl home, and you don't even know her name?" She steps around him with hands on her hips.

Her long black hair flows freely, reaching her mid-back. Her pink kimono is speckled with white flowers, more intricate than the ones worn by the rest of the villagers. Our eyes are locked on each other, and she taps her foot impatiently. "Well Hiroshi, are you going to introduce us?"

"So that's your name, Hiroshi?" I ask.

"Yes, and this is my sister—" His voice wavers.

"Miki. Sorry, my brother is being such a bone-head. He's usually not so impolite. What's your name?"

"My name is...," I almost blurt out Sarah, I bite my tongue to keep the words from passing my lips. Sarah could be dangerous to use. The people of Nihon only have Japanese names from what Mrs. Takara told me. She called me something before bringing me here, Rika I think. Their impatient eyes look me up and down. "My name is Rika," I fumble to say the name correctly.

"Oh, that's so pretty." Miki grabs my hand and pulls me into the hut. "We can't stand outside all night, it's getting cold."

"Okay," I murmur as I allow her to drag me along. The square shape of the one-room hut makes it look bigger from the outside. The log-cabin style structure has a red hue to the grain of the wood, perhaps it was made using cherry trees. There is a stone fire pit in the middle of the room, along with a wood stove made of clay against the wall, and a short wooden table next to it.

"I'll build a fire," Hiroshi says before going back outside.

"Where did you come from? Why have you come to our village? I like the color of your hair, why do you keep it so short?" She riddles me with questions.

"Um."

Hiroshi returns with both arms loaded with firewood, carrying the heavy logs with ease. "Quit pestering her Miki, she's been through enough today. Why don't you leave her alone for the evening so she can rest?"

"Fine, but you're telling me everything in the morning." She reluctantly pulls bedrolls off a nearby shelf. "I'm sorry, we only have two."

"Don't worry, she can use mine," Hiroshi answers while tending to the fire. "Now get to bed." The girl gives him a quick hug and lies down in her bedroll.

Hiroshi then motions for me to follow him. He pulls back the door flap and waits for me to go outside. "Rika, you can tell me if this is none of my business, but Miki did have a point about your appearance. Your reddish brown hair, along with your powers, reminds me of a yokai, but you don't look or smell like any I've ever seen."

"Glad I wore deodorant this morning, wouldn't want to smell like I'm part animal, not that I am." I grimace at my constant awkwardness.

Hiroshi stares up at the stars, trying not to put too much pressure on me I guess.

"I come from a village far away," I lie. "Everyone there has similar hair and has powers." My palms are sweating again. "It's a long story."

"I have heard of villages specializing in unique abilities, and I do like long stories."

"Maybe another time, long story short I ran away from home. Pretty childish isn't it?" That should be believable enough, and partially true. I grip my hands to keep from wringing them nervously. My wound, it's completely healed. I do my best to not let my surprise show on my face.

"I suppose, but if you left for the right reasons you shouldn't hold it against yourself." If he knows I'm lying, he's doing a good job of not letting on. "Let's go to bed, we can discuss these matters at a later time." He holds the door flap open once again.

Miki is already snoring as I go to the bedroll she laid out for me and try to get comfortable.

"Good night," Hiroshi whispers as he tends to the fire.

"Good night, thank you for everything." I close my eyes to sleep, but too many thoughts and questions clutter my mind.

Can I trust these people? So far they've been nice. Hiroshi did rescue me after all. Not to mention these new powers I have. Why didn't they appear on Earth? This world may hold the key that unlocks this inner strength.

How can this all be? And in a world that looks like ancient Japan, yet everyone speaks English, or is everyone speaking Japanese and I magically can too? Wouldn't be too surprising considering the day I've had. My head aches, I suck in a breath of air and slowly blow it out, for now I'll have to rely on the help of a yokai and a little girl.

4

The sweet scent of blueberries surrounds me, opening my eyes I see Mom carrying a tray piled high with blueberry pancakes. I'm in my own bed, soft and warm. It was all a dream. "Mom—"

Screams jolt me truly awake, "What is that?"

Hiroshi rushes to the door. "I'll be back. Miki, take Rika and hide in the cellar." He bursts through the door flap and is gone.

A bell clangs in the distance and Miki clutches my hand. She pulls me to the kitchen area and pushes the table aside to reveal a trap door. She swings the door open, and a musty aroma wafts through the air. We climb down a ladder inside. I close the door and we crouch down. The cellar is nearly pitch-black now with only a few beams of morning light streaming through the cracks of the door. I breathe through my mouth in a futile attempt to avoid the rank air of the cellar.

"A demon has entered the village. The bell warns the villagers and calls the protectors to come and help. Right now Hiroshi is the only protector in this village. He is very strong, and he's usually back fairly soon. There's no need to worry."

The screams fade in a snap, and for a moment everything is still. Until the ground above me begins trembling, shaking dust from the ceiling unto us.

"We need to leave." I grab her hand and we push the trap door open.

We emerge from the hut and freeze, less than a hundred yards in front of us is a giant monster battling Hiroshi. The yokai is probably twice the size of any human, and it's covered in brown hair like a Sasquatch. Its long fangs and sharp claws glimmer in the sunlight; almost nothing about this creature resembles a human. What have I gotten myself into?

Hiroshi bravely stands between us and the Sasquatch. The demon swats Hiroshi out of the way like a bug. He crashes to the ground, but quickly scrambles to his feet.

"I've got to help Hiroshi. Go back inside and wait for me."

My legs can't carry me fast enough. The yokai knocks Hiroshi down again, this time he struggles to force his bruised body off the ground. Hiroshi is powerful and has experience battling yokai, heck he is one, and yet this yokai is giving him a beating. So how is a weakling like me going to stand a chance?

I halt directly behind Hiroshi. A shadow swiftly engulfs us, I arch my neck too see the gigantic demon looming over us. I was wrong, Sasquatch is more than three times Hiroshi's height. Fear spreads through my spine and out to my fingertips, each hair on my arms rising with a jolt.

Hiroshi's tail sways to the right and brushes against my kimono. He spins around to face me. "What are you doing? Get out of here before you get yourself killed." He jumps into the air, higher than anyone I've ever seen, and punches the demon squarely across the jaw. "Run while I distract him." He dodges behind the creature and yanks on its fur.

It would be easy to escape to shelter, to crawl into a hole in the floor, but within the corners of my heart it's clear that if I'm going to survive in this world, I must learn to take action.

I frantically scan the area trying to find anything with which to hit the Sasquatch or to tie him up, yet there is nothing but the open farm field. Hiroshi strikes the demon hard in the back of the head; he stumbles backward, nearly falling on top of Hiroshi. He crashes to the ground.

This is my chance. I climb onto the heaving chest of the monster and slam both of my fists down onto his grotesque fur. Dust and fleas spray into my face, he's not fazed one bit. Why isn't the red light returning?

His jagged talons wrap around my scrawny arms. I cringe at the crack that pangs through the air. Instantly I feel faint.

I squint my eyes closed, waiting to be crushed. Instead, the twangy hairs of his paws brush against my skin as they slide off. I rub my biceps and open my eyes to see Hiroshi hovering over the twisted neck of the Sasquatch.

I tumble off of him. "What did you do?"

"I did what had to be done." He inhales deeply through his nose and closes his eyes, when his eyelids open his eyes are a blood red. He blinks and the abnormal pigment disappears.

My body trembles, my eyes dart from side to side. I have to get out of here. Adrenaline courses through me as I wildly flee the scene. I head for the cherry orchard that sits on the edge of the village.

His rough fingers grab my hand.

"Get away from me!" I scream while ripping away.

"Rika wait you don't understand." He jumps in front of me with inhuman speed, causing me to collide into his brick wall of a chest, knocking the wind out of me.

I gasp for air, shoulders heaving as I attempt to cry.

"No, no, don't do that." He wraps his arms securely around me. "I had to stop him. If I hadn't, he would have simply moved on to the next village seeking out new victims."

I rest my forehead against him. His breath is steady, not at all like my erratic rhythm. I don't know what to think of him. He is a yokai capable of killing, but he did it for the greater good, does that still make him a monster?

"What I'm about to say isn't going to make you like me any better."

I brace myself for the news. He's probably going to tell me he's murdered hundreds.

"I need your help, in killing the princess."

"Kill her!" My voice erupts a little hysterically. I attempt to back away, but he restricts me. The bird yokai called me the princess. There's half a chance he's after me. Keep your cool Sarah. Don't freak out, there's no way that crazy bird is right. I take a deep breath to compose myself. "Why do you want to end her life?"

"This world is dying. The yokai are destroying it one human, one village at a time. The hunger for more power will never be quenched. With every kill a yokai makes he grows stronger. What do you think will happen when the legendary princess is slain and her soul is sucked out? That demon will become the most powerful being Nihon has ever seen. I will use the chance to stop this madness.

If we continue down this senseless path there will be nothing left of Nihon, only bodies and half dug graves. If another yokai takes her strength, there will be no hope for us. It must be me, and I need your help. There are creatures out there stronger than I, ones who have killed hundreds to gain their rank. If I am ever to compete with them I will need help. I want you to join me in my search for the princess."

"How can I be of any use to you?"

He shakes his head, "You discredit yourself. The demonstration you gave in the cherry orchard last night has me convinced you're the key to my success."

"But I can't control these powers, I couldn't even help you just now!"

"The potential is there, you only need to learn to unlock it."

Conspiracy to commit murder, not really my scene. Plus when is Mrs. Takara supposed to show up? Though he has a point, what would be the consequences if a blood thirsty demon slayed the princess seeking to destroy the world? I glance up at his overwhelmingly tall stature, the defining lines of his muscles are unreal. Do I really have a choice in the matter? Either I cast my lot with him, or risk running into another yokai whose intentions aren't so noble. I nod my head. "I'll go with you."

"Great." He prattles on quickly in his excitement, "We can work on your powers, and we'll be the most powerful team that anyone has ever seen. Wait 'till I tell Miki."

"Is it really safe for her to come with us?"

He thoughtfully leans against the scraggly bark of a cherry tree. "She may be young, but she'll surprise you. Though, she'll hate the idea of leaving her home."

He pushes off the tree trunk hastily and grasps onto my hand. In a bubbly mood he bounces slightly with each stride as he leads me back to their hut. "Miki, I have news."

"Hiroshi, you're safe!" She is waiting outside for us, and leaps into his arms "What's the big news?"

He gives a worried sigh before answering her question. "We're leaving."

"*What?*" Miki wiggles from his arms. "We can't leave. This is our home. The new star in the sky means nothing!" Miki backs away from us.

"Miki." He reaches out for her, but she takes another step toward the hut. "We need to find the princess."

"What is your obsession with her? She's probably dead, or just a rumor." Miki's voice grows louder as she becomes more upset. "You're never going to find her!" She stamps her foot, kicking up a small plume of dust.

"Don't you see? We will never be truly safe until the princess is dead, and I have her strength. Please try to understand. I'm doing this for you, for the entire world. We'll leave tomorrow."

That is sudden, shouldn't he give her more time to adjust, for me to adjust? What's the huge rush?

"You can't be serious." Miki's eyes narrow, as if laser beams would spring forth. I pray she never glares at me that way.

Hiroshi throws his hand into the air and roars, "The sign has appeared! We don't have time to be arguing about this, we must find her."

"All this excitement and it isn't even noon." I bend over to eye level with the frustrated little girl. "I'm not thrilled with the idea of hunting down the princess either. It's the only way he knows how to deal with the situation I guess." I put my arm around her shoulders.

She drops her head, her long hair creates a black curtain covering her face, then bursts into tears and hugs me.

"This was my parents' house. I can't leave them," she sobs.

"I'm sorry about your parents." Mom and Dad, do they care I'm gone? Are they still going through with the divorce?

"They died several years ago. Back then, we had several protectors, but they all died in the attack. If Hiroshi hadn't been traveling in the woods nearby on that fateful day, we all would have been slain. The villagers begged Hiroshi to stay and protect them. Ever since, Hiroshi has stayed and taken care of me and the village. He's strong, he doesn't need the princess' powers. We can't leave. What will happen to the village, to my home? What if it's destroyed?" Miki cries even harder, causing her narrow shoulders to shake.

I've got to calm her down, I know how hard it is being taken away from your home without notice. "With more yokai searching for the princess, it won't be safe here. Our best bet is to leave. If you stay instead of losing a house, we might lose you. I understand your parents' home is very important to you, but your life is worth more than all the houses in the world. Please come with us."

Miki pulls her head away slightly, she brushes back her hair and tucks it behind her ear.

"All right, but only because *you* asked." She sniffles and wipes her runny nose on her sleeve. "Maybe we can get one of the neighbors to take care of the house while we're gone. Hey, there's a newlywed couple who are looking for a home. We get a house sitter, and they'll have a place to stay." A smile spreads across her tear stained face.

"I'm sorry for yelling," Hiroshi says, stepping out from behind me. I never heard him circle around; in Mrs. Takara's stories she mentioned yokai share traits similar to the animals they resemble. He's stealthy. While I travel with him I need to learn his strengths, his weaknesses. If we do become enemies, at least then I would stand a chance in defending myself.

33

Miki folds her arms, "You should be, and despite what I think about this whole ordeal, I've decided to go with you." Though content with her decision, she's obviously not too enthused about it.

Getting out of this town before more creatures come out of the woodwork is logically the best thing for me, yet I've hardly a chance to breathe before my life takes another unexpected turn. It will take all that's in me to keep up. Focusing my scrambled thoughts I ask, "Where will we be going?"

"There is a mountain range east of here. If the princess truly has returned she will need to pass through there to return to the castle. That's where we will start our journey." We nod in agreement. We'll soon depart on a mission…to murder an innocent girl.

5

Hiroshi wakes us before dawn. After making the proper arrangements and gathering needed supplies, we depart down the dirt road through town, my eyes are puffy and sore from lack of sleep.

"Good-bye. Thanks for taking care of the house for us. We'll be back soon." Miki's small hand waves good-bye to the young couple and the villagers who have come to wish us farewell. "I'm sure going to miss this place."

Miki continually looks over her shoulder, catching as many glimpses of her home as she can.

The journey ahead will be dangerous. I can't let anything slip about who I really am, or where I'm really from. Those facts alone would qualify for my execution, even though I'm no princess, they would want to make certain.

"How long will it take to get to the castle?" I ask Hiroshi.

"Well, our first stop is Lake Mizumi, we'll need to stop there for fresh water. It's about a day's journey."

We leave the village and follow the dirt path, which leads us into a forest of pine trees. Ruts are cut into the two sides of the road, from carts carrying supplies between towns I would assume.

Twigs snap from within the forest around us, we halt. Branches of a holly bush sway on the left side of the trail. Attempting to retreat I lose my footing, falling right on my bag of supplies.

A small grey rabbit with a fluffy white tail hops across the road and nibbles on the pedals of amethyst wildflowers on the other side. I'm such a klutz.

"Are you okay?" Hiroshi asks while offering his hand.

Though embarrassed, I accept his help. "I'm fine, it's only a rabbit after all." Dusting off my kimono I try not to make eye contact, that would only make me feel worse.

"On the way up we should practice your skills. In case next time we encounter something a bit bigger," he chuckles.

"Very funny, but I will need your help. I didn't know I had these abilities until recently."

"Really? There are cases when powers don't manifest themselves in humans until later. How old are you?"

"Seventeen, why?"

"Curiosity, I've known a couple humans who didn't get their powers until they were adults, it's just not as common. I once knew a man who received his powers at thirty. I guess you can never tell. Be thankful you got yours when you did. On a side note, the princess should be around the same age as you."

I should have lied and told him I was twenty or something. Mrs. Takara told me the princess is the same age as me. This isn't easing any suspicions he may have against me.

"We can use that to our advantage when we encounter the princess. She'd surely run at the sight of me, but she'd trust a girl who's human and similar age. Lulling her into a false sense of security could be our only shot at taking her down. She's more powerful than both of us, even ten of us."

I clear my voice and change the subject, "And how old are you?"

"Nineteen," He replies.

I catch myself thinking of him as dating material. Surprising since he's half lion on a human hunting expedition!

We continue in conversation as the hours pass by, I constantly push the subject back to Hiroshi and Miki so I don't accidently reveal details about myself.

The sun is now setting, and the forest is growing darker every minute. Hiroshi plants both feet firmly on the ground, surveying the tree line of the dense forest. "Let's set up camp. I'll get wood to make a fire. You two stay here."

I shrug the leather bag off my shoulder, and pull out the rice and vegetables Miki and I packed this morning. It's smashed into the burlap cloth wrap, but it should taste the same.

Soon Hiroshi returns with plenty of kindling to get a fire started. "I will get bigger logs to last us through the night. Can you please start a fire, Rika?" He asks, as if I should know.

I can hardly get a fire going with matches and newspaper, let alone sticks. Summer camp sleeping in log cabins, roasting marshmallows, and eating in a recreation hall didn't exactly prepare me for roughing it in the woods.

"Um, not really. I'm really bad at it."

"Miki, will you please help Rika start a fire?"

"Yes sir." Miki salutes Hiroshi. She giggles and sits down next to me, crossing her legs. She hands me a split tree limb with a channel running down the length and a dowel.

I pick up the scraggly sticks covered in moss and place them in a teepee shape, similar to the fires I've seen on TV. I start rubbing the dowel along the tree limb, figuring that if the survival guys on cable can do this, then so can I.

I glance over at Miki; she raises her eyebrows and gives me a perplexed look, but stays seated. She must think I'm an idiot. Fifteen agonizing minutes later, Hiroshi returns with logs for the fire, and I still haven't made anything happen, not a spark, not smoke, nothing.

Hiroshi and Miki look at each other and then at me, he shakes his head and they both burst into laughter. "I can't help her. She is really, really bad at making fires."

Meanwhile I try to ignore the criticism, still hard at work, rubbing two sticks together in the hopes that something magically will happen.

Hiroshi sighs. "Here, let me help you." He sets down the logs and crouches next to me. Grabbing my hands, he starts to instruct me. "You're not pushing hard enough nor fast enough. Make sure the dried moss is close to the end of the groove to allow the sparks to fall on it." After about a minute, the moss catches fire, and soon the fire is ablaze. "See, it's not that hard."

Show off. If I was back home I'd use a lighter, or better yet turn up the furnace.

Seeing my disappointment, he attempts to reassure me, "With a little practice you'll get the hang of it."

Miki pipes in, "What he means is that with lots and *lots* of practice you might get the hang of it."

"Hey, I warned you," I protest, trying to save my dignity.

He places a hand on her shoulder. "Okay, let's stop picking on Rika and eat dinner."

After dinner we roll out our bedrolls around the campfire. Miki plops down hers next to Hiroshi. He lies down on the cold hard ground on the other side of the fire, pulling his brown wool blanket up to his chin.

The bright campfire and lush forest with the heavy scent of pine trees, bring me back to camping with my family when I was a kid, when life was perfect. I wonder how Mom and Dad are doing. They must be so worried. What did they think when I wasn't in bed this morning? Do they think I ran away, or was even kidnapped? My absence is probably adding more stress to their already broken relationship. Will they really go through with the divorce? If I could get back home, there's a chance I could stop it. Perhaps I could reunite our family—

My thoughts are interrupted by a whisper. "Rika?"

I prop myself up on my elbows. "Yes?"

"Can I sleep next to you?"

"I suppose."

Miki grins and moves her bedroll close to mine.

"So now I'm alone over here?" complains Hiroshi.

"Do you want to sleep over here too?" I tease.

"Well, if you insist." He jumps up, grabbing his blanket, and places it on the other side of me.

My heart skips a beat. I had assumed it was Miki he wanted to sleep next to, not me, but here he is, lying only two feet away.

The night grows quiet, with only the distant chirps of crickets singing in the background, and I can hear the sound of his breathing. Wow, I sound like a stalker, but I've never been this close to a sleeping guy before, let alone a completely gorgeous one. I never dreamed of sleeping next to Brandon before, and here I am, next to Hiroshi, who I met only a couple days ago.

Is it weird that I find a man who's half-human half-lion attractive? He doesn't have whiskers, and his face and body are *mostly* human, so it's not *that* strange. My world has been turned upside down, the last thing I should be thinking about is boys. My heart pounds in my chest, deep breaths Sarah. I've got to calm down if I'm ever to fall asleep.

The frigid air wakes me from my shallow sleep. The sun has not yet risen, but the sky is light enough that the stars have disappeared. I roll over to see if anyone else is up, but to my surprise, no one is there. Startled, I scan the campsite to confirm they're gone. Where could they be? They wouldn't have left without telling me, would they?

Calling their names, I search our campsite for clues. Their bags and bedding are still here. Why didn't I hear anything? I'm a heavy sleeper, but sleeping through a kidnapping would be a new record.

I slip on my sandals and charge through the woods along the trail we were following, praying to see any signs of Hiroshi or Miki.

After searching for well over half an hour, a lump forms in my throat. I'm such a failure, maybe they left me. I can't do anything right. I swallow hard, closing my eyes I try to clear my head. Faintly in the distance I hear trickling water, a river! It should lead to the lake; I bet that's where they've gone.

I dart down the dirt path, the sound of rushing water growing louder with each step I take. With excitement my speed increases. I turn a corner and the trees clear. In front of me is a sapphire-blue lake, with a white-pebbled beach. The beauty is breathtaking.

I've made it, yet there's no sign of them. "Hiroshi, Miki, are you there?" I call out, but there is no reply.

Ripples form and waves of water explode from the middle of the lake. Something breaks through the surface of the water. I quickly dive behind a bush. Peering through the leaves, I spy a man trudging out of the lake. He is incredibly short, at best four feet tall, and covered in gray scales; slits on the side of his neck resemble gills. What an ugly little man, he must be some sort of fish yokai.

The fish demon cackles like a hyena before he stalks toward the river.

I push back a fist full of twigs to get a better view, not realizing how fragile they are, one or two snaps apart.

He whips around. "Who's there?"

Now I've done it. I'm going to be his next victim. Crouching down lower, I inhale and exhale as slowly and quietly as possible, being sure not to move a muscle.

He examines the area, walking along the tree line. At last, his webbed feet plant themselves in front of me. The smell of rancid fish and algae emanates from his scaly skin; his breath is heavy and moist.

My heart is pounding right out of my chest, and sweat rolls down my cheek; this is it. Out of nowhere, a cry from the woods attracts his attention, and he rushes through the trees following after the voice.

I let out a sigh of relief and relax my aching muscles. I've never been that scared in my life. He could have taken Hiroshi and Miki. He just came from the lake, I bet that's where he's hidden them. Hopefully they're still alive, and it's not their corpses who great me. After all, who would be alive after being submerged for so long?

To make swimming possible, I remove all the layers of my kimono, all the way down to my blue polka-dot bra and underwear; at least these won't be see-through when I get wet. I poke my head above the green leaves of the bush and make certain the coast is clear before making a mad dash to the lake.

I dive into the freezing cold water and swim to the middle of the lake, trying not to think about what will happen when the fish returns. I duck my head underwater, nothing but a murky blackness below me.

I come up to the surface, gasping for air. My legs tremble with fatigue, the chill of the water causes me to shiver; panic sets in. The fish yokai will be back any moment now, and I still can't find them! If I don't turn back to shore soon I'll drown, and the yokai won't matter anymore. But if I leave now I may never find them. With one last desperate attempt to find my friends, I plunge under the water. Surveying the area I can't see anything more than water and algae.

At the brink of giving up, a glitter in the water catches my eye. I swim closer, tiny bubbles float up from below.

I'm on to something. Ignoring the numbness in my toes, I return to the surface to fill my lungs with air before seeking out the source of the bubbles. As I dive deeper and deeper through the murky water, a strange blue light becomes visible emanating from a giant bubble. Getting closer, I see that there are people inside.

The bubble is large and intimidating, about the size of a house. Urgently I seek a way in. My lungs are burning and feel as if they will explode. Seeing no other option, I thrust my hand in, hoping to pop it. Instead of bursting, the walls of the blue bubble ooze around my hand, carefully allowing me to enter without letting the water in. I fall into the bubble, coughing out water and inhaling deeply.

There are over a dozen people sprawled out on the floor, some even piled on top of each other, yet they are all asleep.

Cautiously stepping around the array of bodies, the floor flexes underfoot, like a bouncy house. I search through the bodies for Miki and Hiroshi. I find Miki half buried under a woman's arm. Flopping the appendage off her, I try to pull her up, but an orange slime causes my hands to slip off. What is this? "Wake up Miki. We have to leave." I shake her shoulders, but she doesn't respond.

I give up for the moment to search for Hiroshi. After checking just about every person I spot his golden hair. He's passed out, his body covered in the orange mucous as well. "Hiroshi." I brush the lock of hair strewn across his face.

Miki lets out a groan, and I run to her side; maybe she's come to. When I reach her it's clear she is still unconscious. I've got to get her out of here before the yokai comes back. There's a chance I can return for the others once she's safe.

Grabbing Miki's limp body by her kimono, I swing her onto my back. Hanging onto her is like holding a greased pig, but somehow I manage to carry her to the edge of the bubble where I entered. Extending my hand to press through the wall, it stretches around my hand, not allowing me through. Oh no! I've got to get us out of here!

Before I can come up with a plan, I'm overwhelmed by the smell of rotting fish, and a thick, moist breath is blowing on my neck. Taking a deep breath, I turn around.

Before my eyes confirm my fears, I already know who it is— the fish yokai. He's inches away from me, the individual gray scales glitter on his skin.

The foul smell of his breath overwhelms me. "You thought you could come into my home and steal from me?" The fish gives a crooked smile, his solid black eyes twinkle with delight. He snatches my wrists with his rough scaly hands. I brace myself for a fight, but instead, he opens his mouth and sings. His tune is soft and sweet, a lullaby.

Miki suddenly feels ten times heavier. I drop her, hoping to struggle free but the yokai just smiles, not stopping his tune for a moment.

He continues to hold tightly. His voice is soothing, the soft notes dance from his tongue, the words indistinguishable. My efforts are in vain as my body becomes weaker and slower. Where is that red light that always helps at a time like this? My eyelids are heavy, and my arms can no longer move.

At the brink of losing consciousness, I spot something moving in the background. I drop to the floor, my body numb. Fighting to keep my eyes open, I barely make out a familiar figure, it's Hiroshi! He's fighting the fish demon.

With all my might, I force myself to stand up, desperate to help. Knees buckling under my own weight, I involuntarily lean against the side of the bubble for support. My hands and feet tingle and burn as I regain feeling in my extremities.

If I'm fast enough, I can sneak up and attack the fish yokai from behind while he's distracted. I quietly negotiate around bodies to the fish demon, but as I lift my foot to kick him, he turns and snatches me into his arms.

45

"You should be dying!" he yells into my face while violently shaking me. The smell alone is enough to make me want to vomit, not to mention the thrashing my head is taking. To my relief Hiroshi hits the creature with one final blow. The demon's eyes roll back into his skull, releasing me and falling to the ground. The body bubbles and oozes through the floor. That is disgusting. Hiroshi kneels down, his eyes a glaring red. He blinks and once again his eyes are normal.

Someone next to me yawns and sits up. I hurry to Miki just as her eyes flutter open.

"Rika?" Miki asks. "I'm so glad to see you. I had this terrible dream. Hiroshi and I went to catch fish in the nearby river for breakfast, and then this ugly fish attacked. Hiroshi was unconscious, and the fish captured me…" She slowly stops speaking, finally realizing where she is. "It wasn't a dream at all, was it?"

I shake my head in reply.

"Then I really was kidnapped. Oh Rika. I'm so glad to see you. Where's Hiroshi? Is he all right? Is the yokai gone?"

"Yes, I'm fine." He pulls Miki into his arms. "The fish yokai is dead. We're safe now. I'm so sorry about all of this." His jaw clenches in frustration. "That slippery creep snuck up behind me. I need to be more careful, better prepared. I don't know what I'd do if anything ever happened to you." He smooths out her messy hair, he must really care about her.

"Guys, worry about apologizing later. We need to get out of here. This bubble let things in, but not out." I push my hand against the wall to demonstrate.

"Hmm, that is a problem." Hiroshi says while pushing on the bubble. "I have an idea, but everyone must be awake and ready to swim before I try."

"I will go check on everyone." Miki eagerly leaps to her feet. After making the rounds she returns. "Everyone is ready."

"All right everyone," Hiroshi calls out in a loud voice. "I'm going to attempt cutting through the bubble with my claws, and with any luck it will tear, allowing us to swim to shore. Is everyone ready?" The group nods in agreement. Hiroshi raises his hand; razor-like claws extend from the end of each finger. He swings at the side of the bubble. With one blow, it shreds and water surges in. The claws retract under his normal fingernails.

We all attempt to swim through the opening, fighting against the current. As the bubble fills with water, the current dies down and we are able to swim out and up to the surface of the lake.

My legs wobble as I trudge up the shore. "We should get back to camp to ensure our gear is still there," I say breathlessly while wringing out my hair and shaking off the water droplets from my arms.

"Wait," Hiroshi sloshes in the water toward me, "Rika, where are your clothes?" He's blushing and won't look at me.

Remembering I'm only in my bra and underwear, my face grows hot with embarrassment. I attempt to cover myself with my hands, one in front of my chest, the other shielding my underwear, though it doesn't do much good. "Oh, yes, my clothes. You see, when I suspected you were in the lake, I removed as much clothing as I could so that it would be easier to swim. Um, I'll go get dressed now."

47

I rush behind the bushes concealing my clothes and begin to redress, but Miki chases after me. "Wait until you've dried off, you'll get your kimono soaking wet."

I glance over at Hiroshi, who quickly averts his eyes, as if he wasn't trying to catch a peek. "I'll make a fire and fetch our things," he says, before awkwardly coughing to clear his throat.

Once Hiroshi and the remaining villagers are gone, I cautiously step out from behind the bush, and we huddle around the fire for warmth. Miki undresses and hangs her clothes on a branch near the fire. "You should hang up your undergarments too so they can dry," she says.

I comply with a nod. I never realized how wonderful the warmth of a fire could be until being freezing cold and buck naked. I relax a bit, allowing the heat to seep in.

"I've returned with our things." Hiroshi emerges from the woods.

"Eeeek!" Miki and I both scream, scrambling to the nearest bush.

"Why didn't you warn us!" Miki shouts.

"Why aren't you wearing any clothes?" Hiroshi retorts. He retreats backwards and trips over a log, crashing into a thorny bush. He yelps and roars, dropping the supplies on the ground so he can pull himself out.

"Go away," Miki demands.

"Fine, a lot of thanks I get after hauling everything." He returns to the forest without further argument.

48

When we can no longer hear his footsteps, we run to the pile and pull out our blankets. Now we at least have something to cover us up. I can't believe he saw me, naked! I wish there was a way to scrub that image from his brain.

It takes hours for our clothes to dry. Miki and I redress, and enter the forest to bring Hiroshi back. Barely setting foot into the tree line, we find him leaning against a tall fir tree. I glance at Miki, and we share a skeptical look.

"You can go dry yourself by the fire now. Come on Miki, let's search for berries, I think I saw some this morning back along the path." I take her hand and march away.

Hiroshi lightly tugs on my sleeve. "My clothes are almost dry, why don't you stay here?" Is it just me or does he get close to me every time he gets the chance?

"All right," Miki groans.

"You shouldn't have been so comfortable earlier. The villagers we saved are a short distance away." Hiroshi smirks.

"What?" My mouth drops.

"Yep, you're lucky I'm the only one that walked over here. They're refugees from a nearby village under attack by yokai."

"We have to help them." Miki perks up.

"I don't know if we really have the time. I'd like to help, but getting to the princess is our priority."

Miki sighs, "The princess again, the unattainable unicorn. These people are real and they need help now. We're going."

49

I chime in, "I agree, we need to assist them. Besides, they may have information on the princess. Just because you think she's going to the castle doesn't mean that's where she'll be."

"Alright then." His face is stern.

We all take a seat around the fire, and I change the topic, "How *did* you save us back there?"

"You mean my incredible strength?"

"No," I chuckle. "You were asleep, under the fish yokai's spell, covered in goo."

"That goo was our souls dissolving. If a yokai has the ability, and time, to "soak the soul" as they call it, rumor has it the powers absorbed are doubled. I'm not exactly sure how I woke up. Only that I thought I heard you say my name, and then I was able to move again."

"Oh, I see." I reply.

"Did you gain any special abilities?" Miki asks excitedly.

"Not sure, let's see if I got the fish's ability to sing," Hiroshi jokes. He clears his throat. A sound similar to a howling dog emerges from his mouth.

Miki covers her ears, "You definitely did not get the gift of singing." She fidgets uncomfortably. "Hiroshi, maybe it's not such a great idea that we search for the princess," she interrupts while fumbling her thumbs and staring at the ground. "I mean, what was so wrong with staying home and protecting the village, like we always do?"

He rolls his eyes, "We've gone over this. The princess' time is up, she's reached her deadline. The new star is signaling us to take action to save Nihon."

"That's not true! The prophecy says the new star means she will return to Nihon and usher in a new era for our world. It's not like she's been around." She crosses her arms, jutting out her jaw in defiance.

Hiroshi's voice raises, "She's had her chance, for 15 years we've been waiting. She could have returned years ago. She's a coward who deserves to die. Her death is eminent, I have to be the one to cast the final blow, or some vile creature will become the supreme being on this planet and kill everyone."

Her eyes become misty as she tries to hold back tears. "I understand, but I still think this is wrong, and if she did return years ago there's no telling where she'll be."

I'm not throwing out my opinion, this whole mission isn't my cup of tea either, but the thought of angering him makes me cringe. Those claws of his are sharp, and his enormous muscles are a constant reminder that he can overpower me in a matter of seconds. If I keep my mouth shut I may have a shot at finding safer company.

6

"I'm so excited to go to Heiwa," Miki sings, skipping along the path. She continues in her sing-song voice, "The village is renowned as being one of the most peaceful. Last time I visited they had a parade, and everyone there was so nice. Too bad we're going on such grim circumstances."

She performs several pin straight cartwheels before bouncing to a round off with impeccable technique. The refugees have made camp up the road, too frightened to go any further.

"Look!" Miki exclaims waving her arms and pointing. "There's the gate to the village!" She races ahead.

Hiroshi turns to me with a smile. Then with his wink, we chase after her. Giggling, I pound my legs faster to keep up with him. "You are going slow on purpose, I know you're faster than that," I accuse. So absorbed in each other, we nearly crash into Miki. "Stop!" I yell, barely in time. I dig my heels into the packed dirt, skidding to a halt.

Miki is frozen in front of the closed large wooden doors. "The gates are never shut." Her normally chipper voice is sullen and quiet. Stunned, she remains motionless as Hiroshi and I push against the weathered wooden panels. I suppose she wasn't prepared to see her treasured memory shattered. The streets are barren, broken pottery shards line the edges of the street, and it's eerily silent. A knot clenches in my stomach.

I pull Miki through the ghost town. Huge cracks have split open the path, and huts lean to the side, threatening to collapse. "It looks like the aftermath of an earthquake." I mumble.

"This was no earthquake," Hiroshi replies grimly. "The stench of yokai is everywhere." Hiroshi tilts his head downward while bending over, sniffing close to the ground. Following a scent trail he steps inside an abandoned hut.

"Ah!" a voice cries out. "Get out!" she croaks. An elderly woman emerges from the hut, swinging her broom.

Hiroshi objects, "Wait, you don't understand. We can help." The old woman lifts her broom and bops him, right on the head. "Ow! What was that for?" Her eyes focus, she takes aim, lifting her broom higher this time.

I step between them. "Stop!" I plead while guarding Hiroshi.

"A human. What are you doing here? Are you with him?" She points her crooked, spindly finger at Hiroshi.

"We heard about your plight from villagers who escaped. What happened?"

She lowers her weapon. "We were experiencing minor earthquakes, but we thought nothing of it. It wasn't until our crops began to die and our food kept disappearing, that we finally realized what was going on, but by then it was too late. The moles had already built an underground network of tunnels, and there was nothing that could be done to stop them. Most people packed up and left, but there are a few of us who have enough courage to stay and fight the varmints."

"What can we do to help?" I ask the woman.

"Isn't it obvious? Get rid of the rodents. The entrance to their underground tunnels is located due north of the village. Let me show you." The old woman picks up a lantern hanging next to the doorway, and leads the way.

Miki's initial shock dissipates, finally able to walk without my guidance. Passing by the empty homes and shops, personal belongings long since deserted remain in doorways. They left so much in their haste.

A black-haired doll lies face down in a mud puddle. I reach for it, but withdraw my hand. We will bring peace back to Heiwa, and the little girl who owns this doll will come back for it.

After making our way through the crumbling town, we come to a large dirt field. Shriveled plants and abandoned farm equipment speckle the ground. Giant mounds of soil dot the landscape. "That's the entrance," she points to a gaping hole. "If you can lure them out we'll handle things from there. Take this, you'll need it to see in the pit." Her shaky hands strike two stones together, sending out sparks and igniting the wick. She hands the lit lantern to me.

"We won't let you down," I assure her. My voice is steady, but the back of my mind fills with doubt, I'm no savior. I'm just a nerdy girl who reads about grand adventures in books. I even signed up for a psychology program to learn how people think. That way I would know how to make the kids at school interested in me, so they'd like me. My last ditch effort to fit in, too bad that isn't going to happen.

"May the ancestors guide your way. I will wait here and stand guard." She grips tightly to the stick of her broom, cracking her knobby knuckles.

Carefully, we climb down the damp soil into the tunnel of perpetual darkness.

The lamp provides a warm glow, illuminating a few feet of the coffee ground like floor in front of me. My right hand holds the lamp while my left traces along the wall, feeling my way through the corridors. Coats of dirt and dust cover my hand, hindering my sense of direction.

After several minutes we come to a fork in the road. "Which way should we go?" I hold the light up to each tunnel.

"I don't know," Hiroshi answers. "We'll have to choose one." Before we have a chance to decide, the tunnel starts to quake.

"What was that?" I raise the lantern as high as my arm will reach. Miki steps behind me. Loud squeaking and rumbling precedes the several mole demons that race out of the tunnel on the right. The yokai halt directly in front of us.

The creatures are on all four legs, yet their size is that of a car. One of them rises to his stubby hind legs. "What are you doing here? Did you think you could convince us to leave?" The mole yokai mocks. "You'd better think again." The leader swats with his paw, signaling the others to attack.

Hiroshi blocks them from charging Miki and me, but in the heat of the moment, I flinch and drop the lantern. I gasp as the glass shatters against the floor, the tunnel flashes pitch-black.

Miki snatches my hand and we back away, dirt and fur engulf us. We scream, but the yokai already has us.

"Hiroshi!" Miki cries. "Help us!"

"I'm coming!" Hiroshi shouts, breathing heavily.

But how long will that take? I latch onto the arm of the mole and jerk away, but his paws refuse to budge. With each tug my determination grows. Energy wells up inside me; until a red glow bursts from my hands.

The mole screeches, releasing us, and it scampers away.

"Are you two all right?" Hiroshi's familiar voice inquires.

"Yes, we're fine. Are there anymore?" I reply out of breath.

"I killed the others who attacked us, but deeper within the tunnels there are sure to be more. There's only one way to find out."

"But Hiroshi, we can't see anything," I point out. "How are we supposed to defend ourselves?"

"Correction, *you* can't see. I can see just fine."

"I thought lions could only see in the dark when there is a bit of light present."

"Yokai tend to have greater abilities than our animal counter parts. Besides, after absorbing the spirit of the mole, my hearing has become better, making it easier to tell where I'm going."

Was it a special ability from the mole demon, or are all his senses becoming keener with each kill?

"Don't worry, I'll guide you. If you'd like, we can all hold hands so that we stick together. Would that make you feel better?"

"As a matter of fact, it would." Only in the sense we won't be separated. My stomach flip flops at the thought of how easily he can murder me. Good thing he's not out for my life, I think. I shudder at the thought.

He grabs my hand, and I hold on to Miki's. His hand is firm but gentle, lessening my fears, for the moment anyway. He leads the way, and Miki trails behind me. We wind our way through the tunnels, completely disorienting me.

After a few minutes more, I hear scratching noises. Turning a corner I collide into Hiroshi. "Why have you stopped?"

"Shh!" His dirty hand covers my mouth. "Too late, run!" Hiroshi races backward, dragging me and Miki along. My arms are yanked so hard they might be ripped from their sockets. I lock my fingers around Miki's and hold on for dear life. Darting through the tunnels left and right, their footsteps are right behind us.

Finally, beams of sunlight stream into the tunnel up ahead. It's the exit! Daylight, sweet daylight, how I've missed you. Hiroshi throws us out of the darkness. I land on my bum, and Miki falls on top of me.

The pack of yokai stampede out of the tunnel. My eyes take several moments to adjust, but once they do I see the moles squinting, covering their faces with their fuzzy paws.

"Leave this village. Your business is done here. You have ruined all of the crops, and there are not enough villagers to replant them. Go now, or else." Hiroshi's voice booms, but the moles burst into laughter.

Their eyes adjust enough for the group to move into an attack formation. The leader shifts his weight to his hind legs, preparing to signal the attack, but beams of light shine in his eyes. More and more rays of white light spread across the moles, focusing on their eyes. "The light! I can't see! It's too bright!" They cry out.

Where is it coming from? I turn around to see the villagers holding rounded mirrors, angling them to use the sunlight as a weapon. Two of the yokai violently gnash their teeth at us, Hiroshi extends his claws and beheads them both simultaneously. The leader drops on all fours and they retreat into the forest without further complaint.

"Woohoo!" Everyone cheers, jumping up and down, and embracing each other. The refugees are among the crowd.

The old woman with the broom approaches us. "Thank you, there is no way to express the service you've done for us. Handsome and brave, he's a keeper." She flashes me a wink, causing her wrinkles to crease deeper. "Let's get back to the village, you deserve some rest."

"Before we head back we need to cover up the tunnel entrance, and any other holes to discourage them from returning." Hiroshi comments. "We will join you later."

"All right, we'll see you soon." She waves good-bye as she and most of the villagers go back to town. A few young men stay to assist us in the grueling task ahead.

Hauling soil and rock from the mounds and filling the holes is backbreaking work. Hiroshi digs into the ground with his claws, scooping up the dirt and flinging it into the holes, while the rest of us use shovels provided by the young men helping. Hiroshi's strength and speed allow him to outperform all of us combined.

The sky above is streaked in a purple haze by the time we are done. Being so tired, no one says a word during the trip back to town. My neck, back, hands, everything hurts. I'm completely filthy, covered from head to foot. Trudging into town, people swarm around us. Their bright smiling faces thank us for helping them. This is a much different atmosphere than earlier today. Paper and glass lanterns are lit through town.

"You have helped us so much, and now we want to repay you. We have brought you the food and supplies we can spare. It's not much, but it's the best we can do," the old woman rejoices in our victory, but her voice has a hint of sadness.

"This is great! I'm starving." Miki rubs her tummy. "It's been such a long day I haven't eaten since breakfast."

"What are we waiting for? Bring the food." The old woman waves her hand, and two young maidens bring out a large bamboo tray filled with food. "Now, come here and have a seat. We have another gift for you."

Sitting down on the split log bench, I gaze at the plethora, sweet buns, exotic fruit, hunks of pork– a feast. My mouth waters and I wipe my hands on my kimono in a futile effort to clean them. After inhaling several mouthfuls of food, I slow down. Trying to be more proper, I look around to complement them on the food, but to my surprise, the villagers are gone. Is this some sort of trap? My muscles tense, preparing for another fight.

The beating of drums thunders from the east. Miki flies off the bench ecstatically. She eagerly watches down the main path of the village. "It's a parade!" She bounces up and down.

Dancers prance around to the beat of the pounding drums. They twirl their hands and weave through patterns around each other. There are only five people, but they improvise well.

The atmosphere is happy and carefree; I'm almost able to forget about the life I should have had back on Earth. My identity crises, even the yokai fade away, though one is sitting right beside me.

Before long, the procession is over, no surprise since so many people are gone. A villager brings us two burlap bags with straps like a backpack, one contains food, the other supplies like medicine, bandages, and a collapsible paper lantern.

This place is wonderful, couldn't we stay here for a few days? My body and soul yearn for a break.

Hiroshi, noticing the expression of regret on my face, attempts to comfort me, "I know it would be nice to stay awhile with them, but we have a mission to complete. Once we have found the princess, we can stay wherever we want."

"What you mean to say is, we will be able to return home first and then go visit places whenever we want," Miki explains to him in a teasing but serious manner.

"Miki, how long have you been away from home before?"

"Not long, only a few days at most."

"I'm sorry Miki. You must be homesick," empathizing with her struggle I squeeze her in close.

"It's nothing. I'm fine." She gives a reassuring smile.

Hiroshi takes Miki's dainty hand. "We can stay here for the night if that is your wish."

I hold my breath, waiting for her answer.

"Yes please, but we'll need to leave tomorrow. The sooner we find the princess, the sooner we can go home."

7

Leaving Heiwa was harder than I had anticipated. The accommodations there were upscale compared to camping on the side of the road. They gave us our own hut to use for the night, the warmth allowed me to sleep in.

Normally a good night's rest will put me in the best of moods, but hitting the road again so soon is killing my feet, and my attitude. These trails can be pretty sketchy; in areas it narrows to only one person wide. Miki and Hiroshi aren't fazed by the constant hiking, whereas my suburbanite life has made me soft. All day long we walk, and walk, and walk some more.

"Once we've reached the top of the hill we'll need to be on the lookout for two reasons: one, the area up ahead is known for bandits, and two, we are getting closer to the castle. We don't want to give our position away, so please no more talking. If you absolutely need to say something, whisper." Hiroshi instructs in a hushed voice. Barely cresting the hill, he lifts his hand signaling us to stop. "Something's coming."

In a split second, the wind is knocked out of me. My head throbs, what happened? Dazed, I slide my arm next to me to prop myself up, but I'm pinned down.

It seems far away but I can hear Hiroshi call out my name, then he begins talking in a different direction, "Okami? Is that really you?" Am I dreaming, or is there someone else here?

"Who wants to know? Wait, Hiroshi?" an unfamiliar voice replies.

"Yes, I can't believe it. How many years has it been?"

"Six or seven, I think."

Blinking open my eyes, I stare straight up to see a wolf yokai. His hair is gray, about chin length, but no wrinkles mar his face. He's un-kempt, his face is smudged with dust, a scraggly beard poking through.

"It's so good to see you."

The wolf demon sits up and squares his shoulders, still straddling me, and Hiroshi pats him on the back. "Why did you sneak up on us like that? And poor Rika, what was that for?"

"You of all people should know I'm searching for the princess. Since she's with you, I'm assuming she isn't the princess, right?" Okami lurks over me again, his crystal blue eyes search mine, down to my soul.

"No, she's not. I found her in an orchard about to be slain by a bird demon. She's only recently discovered her

63

abilities. Definitely not powerful enough to be the princess."

My pathetic nature is helping for once, I did drop out of the sky unexpectedly exactly when the princess should have. Could I be her? If I was it would lead to instant death. No I can't be her, that's so ridiculous.

"So are you two...juji?"

"No, no, no, we're just friends."

Still trapped under the burly wolf yokai, I crane my neck to whisper to Miki, "What's juji?"

"It means engaged, promised. You know, you two would be good for each other." Miki replies in a hushed tone, giggling under her breath.

"Okay, if you say so," Okami replies rolling his eyes, he's not convinced. "Are you on your way to the palace?"

"Yes, it's the first place she would go."

"My thinking as well. Care to join me on the trip, it should only take us about a day to get there?"

"Of course Okami, the more of us, the better chance we have at capturing the princess. If her powers are half of what they're rumored to be, we'll need all the help we can get."

Hiroshi may be the leader of our group, but I don't agree with his decision. This guy is creepy. He has sharp teeth, a snaggletooth that hangs over his bottom lip even when his mouth is closed, and at each fingertip two inches of black claws are constantly extended; not to mention his big bushy wolf tail. Although his appearance of animal to human is proportional to Hiroshi, his demeanor leaves much to be desired.

Finally Hiroshi notices my look of distaste, and he elbows Okami.

"Oh, sorry about that. I didn't mean to hurt *you*. What was your name again?" His grumbly voice lacks sympathy. As he releases me, he rises to standing, hovering over me for a moment, before stepping away.

"It's Rika," I reply haughtily. Still lying on the ground, I'm not at all amused by his pathetic apology.

"Rika, I will try to remember. Sorry about that." Nothing about this guy is genuine, not his fake smile or his apology, my instincts tell me he's trouble.

Okami offers his hand to help me up, I reluctantly take it. As his hand wraps around mine, the rough calluses scratch against my soft skin. His abrasive skin mirrors his personality.

"This is Miki. She's like a sister to me," Hiroshi introduces.

"Glad to meet you, Miki." Contrary to my reaction, she's not put off by him at all.

"Okami, you've been there before, so lead the way," Hiroshi instructs. This better not be a precursor to him assuming leadership over all of us. No, Hiroshi wouldn't let that happen, would he? We'll split up after searching the castle anyways.

Okami scratches his scruffy chin with his claws, "I haven't been there in quite some time, but I should be able to find it without too much trouble."

Traveling to the castle, Hiroshi and Okami catch up on the past few years. Throughout most of the conversation Okami boasts about his physical prowess and how he strikes fear into the lowly humans.

That night, we camp off the main trail near a babbling stream. Laying out our bedrolls, Hiroshi has one as well. "Where did you get that?" I ask while flattening out the wrinkles in my bed.

"It was in the bag of supplies from Heiwa." He waves it up into the air to unroll it.

"Nice, way better than the sleeping on grass." I smooth out my blankets.

Okami plops down on the ground. "Uh, it's just fabric. I haven't had one in years. The less I need to haul around with me, the better" He turns up his nose, that guy is stuck-up for being a slob.

Hiroshi defensively taunts Okami, "Come on, you can't tell me that even a big strong demon like yourself doesn't enjoy comfort once in a while."

The grey hairs on Okami's arms stand on end.

Sensing the tension growing, I intervene, "Yes, well, we should have dinner and get some rest. We've got a big day ahead of us tomorrow." The thought of food allows everyone to calm down a bit.

Miki sleeps next to me, as usual, but Hiroshi and Okami are on the other side of the fire. I guess Hiroshi doesn't want to appear weak by sleeping next to girls. Part of me is relieved not to be unconscious next to a yokai, but there's also a hint of regret, if I wasn't from Earth, I could date him without fear of being mistaken for the princess and murdered. Maybe even have a life with him. What am I saying, he would never date me, princess or not. I'm not worth dating, the guys back on Earth proved it. Besides he's a potential murderer! I toss and turn, attempting to get him out of my head, but it's useless.

The next morning, I awake to something bumping my bedroll. "Cut that out," I whine while rolling over, but I'm kicked hard. "Ouch! I said to cut that out!" I raise my voice as I sit up to confront the culprit.

Okami glares down at me. "She's up. I told you I could persuade her to rise before sunup, now we can get going."

"You! You can't do that to someone," I say, gritting my teeth, clenching my fists, my nails driving into my palms.

"I can, and I just did," Okami sneers and turns his back.

Anger spreads throughout my body, overtaking me. I leap to my feet and charge, knocking him to the ground. "You can't do that to *me*. I don't care who you think you are."

Okami rolls over. I grab a fist full of sandy soil and I rub it in his eyes. He slaps me across the cheek, so I punch him in the jaw.

He's about to strike me back, when Hiroshi grabs Okami's fist, only inches away from my face. "Knock it off."

Reluctantly, Okami relaxes his hand and lowers his arm. He shoves me away, and stomps off to pout, his wolf tail swings haughtily back and forth.

Miki rushes to check on me. "Are you okay?" She examines my cheek. "I don't think it will bruise. He really wanted to get going this morning and didn't want to wait for you. I'm sorry."

She helps me to my feet, behind her I hear Hiroshi berating Okami, "Take it easy…"

Miki tries to change the subject. "Come on, breakfast is ready. Food makes everything better."

We eat without speaking a word, and continue on. I hope that creep is happy. We are back on our way to the castle, to find her highness. Well, I am lucky he didn't kill me when he had the chance.

Several hours of silence pass by. Deep in thought about home, I fail to notice a pot hole in the road. I stumble, and swiftly Hiroshi catches me in his arms. He looks down at me, so similar to the moment we first met. His eyes are so warm. Still holding tightly to me, he opens his mouth to speak, but a loud disapproving grunt from Okami ruins the moment.

We continue on for hours, skipping lunch at Okami's demand. As the hours pass by, Miki becomes hangry. "How far away is this castle? Shouldn't we be getting close? You said it was only a one-day journey."

"We would be there by now if you didn't walk so slow." He talks tough, but the wavering in his voice isn't reassuring.

She folds her arms in disgust, I think she's finally starting to see why I dislike him.

We press on, even though Miki's stomach growls louder every minute. After another hour, Hiroshi insists we stop. He and Okami hunt for food while Miki and I prepare the fire. They return with a creature that resembles a wild pig. Okami thrusts the animal over his shoulder and tosses it to the ground, smiling at his accomplishment, though he seems more pleased with the kill than with the fact we have food.

Hiroshi leaves Okami to tend to the meat, standing behind me he says, "Would you like to go for a walk? I know we've been hiking all day, but there is something I'd like to show you." He waits patiently for my reply.

I spin around on my bum. Yes, I'd love to stroll around some more in these sandals that do nothing to support the arch of my feet, causing them to ache incessantly, and I'll have flat feet by the time we make it to the castle. Not to mention the blisters!

Although I say nothing, he looks me over, the bags under my eyes, my swollen ankles, he sees it all. "I can carry you if you're tired." His golden eyes plead with me.

How can I say no to that? "A change of scenery would be nice." I glance over at Okami gutting the animal.

"Wonderful," he grabs my hand, pulls me onto his back, and we're off. "Hold on tight. If I run it will only take a minute."

"Okay." I wrap my arms around his neck, attempting to hang on without strangling him.

"Here we go." He picks up the pace.

Giggles bubble up inside, this is this most fun I've had since I've been here. The piggy-back ride is a little awkward since my kimono doesn't allow my legs to wrap around him, making me practically kneel on his back, but it's still great. All too soon we break through the tree line, arriving at the edge of a cliff.

He takes a knee and slides me off. "I came across this while we were tracking the boar."

"It's amazing!" The cliff opens up to a beautiful view of the clear blue sky above, the snowy mountains in the distance, and the lush green valley below dotted with wildflowers. The horizon is far off in the distance, the great expanse takes my breath away. We've been traveling through densely packed forests, the sudden openness makes me light headed.

He confidently perches at the edge of the cliff, his legs dangling off, and he waves for me to join him.

I've always been terrified of heights, even in tall buildings with glass windows and railings to keep me from falling– here there's nothing. My heart races as I edge myself closer to him. Cautiously I take a seat slightly behind him, so I won't have to peer over the edge. My throat is tight with anxiety, my voice cracks, "Thank you for bringing me here."

"Relax, you'll be fine. I'll save you if you fall." He takes a deep breath, admiring the vista. He slides his hand close to mine, enough for our fingertips to brush.

My heart races again, but not out of fear this time.

"I'm sorry about the trouble with Okami, he's a lot different than I remember. When we were kids we used to play together all of the time. He was my best friend, and one of the nicest people you could meet."

"What happened to him?"

"I don't know, it's baffling how much he's changed. Last I heard from him he left to train with a master fighter when we were still young. We both wanted to be the strongest and someday obtain the princess's powers."

"Hunting down and murdering an innocent person doesn't sound like something a nice person would do."

"True, but I'm doing it to help people. Okami said that's what he wants as well, but I'm not too sure anymore. He's become harsh and greedy." Carefully he scoots in closer to me and places his arm around my shoulders.

My cheeks burn with embarrassment, I'm so glad he can't see me from this angle.

"I promise I won't let him hurt you again, and I will try my best to keep him away from you altogether. I would ask him to part ways with us, but I'm worried what would happen if Okami found the princess before us. For now, we need to put up with him, are you ok with that?"

"I'll live."

"You're great." He wraps his other arm around me, embracing me, my heart pounds faster still, I feel as if I'll have a heart attack.

I don't know how he feels about Rika, but if he knew I'm really Sarah he may have other thoughts about me. This all too sobering thought allows me to breathe easy again, slowing my pulse. "We should return to camp."

"You're right. I neglected to tell anyone where we're going, and the others might be a little suspicious. Miki already wants me to ask you on a date–" He pulls away quickly, his face red. "I mean…" He obviously didn't intend to let that slip.

"No worries, she's a sweet kid." I brush it off, trying not to entertain the idea of us being romantic. Probably thinks of me as a sister too. "Before we return there's something I would like to tell you."

"You can be honest with me." He leans in close again, propping his shoulder against mine.

No I can't. "When I ran away from home, it was because my parents' marriage was falling apart. My dad had an affair, and was leaving us. I had worked very hard for my future, and suddenly my mom wanted to send me away. So I left, exactly what my mom wanted, just not precisely where she expected."

"I see. Do you wish to return home?"

"At times, but it's impossible."

"Give it time, you'll patch things up with them eventually."

"I hope you're right."

He takes my hand and carries me back to camp. Upon returning, Miki is whispering to Okami. They stare at us with curious eyes.

"Lovely weather today." Miki purses her lips, trying to keep a straight face.

"Oh cut it, where were you two?" Okami interjects.

"We were at the cliff side," Hiroshi answers.

"You weren't gone for very long. I guess it wasn't that impressive. Is that why you didn't bring us with you?" Miki complains.

"No, after what happened this morning I wanted to give Rika a break."

"Right…" Okami cocks an eyebrow. "That still doesn't explain why Miki didn't go. If you want to go on a date, I'm not going to stop you." He flicks his hand in the air. "Just tell me next time so I know to keep a closer eye on Miki, and you said you weren't juji."

"It wasn't a date." I blurt out.

He smirks. "Whatever."

I spend the rest of our lunch in strained silence, I'm too aggravated with Okami to have a civilized conversation with anyone. Everyone else peaceably enjoys talking of the past, present, and future. Even Okami is swept away in chit chat, but all too soon he orders us to march onward. Cedar, pine, noble fir, redwood, every kind of evergreen imaginable is contained within this forest, and I thought the cherry orchard was never ending.

The width of the trail widens to fork in the road. The hot afternoon sun beats down on our heads. I scratch my scalp, I'm destined to get a sunburn, my fair skin isn't meant to be outdoors without copious amounts of sunblock and a hat. My only saving grace is the trees provide shade most of the time. The freckles on my face are sure to multiply, last summer they spread to my eyelids and lips, thank goodness they faded over the winter.

I'll see what camping all summer does for my complexion. Miki has a darker skin tone than I do, she probably doesn't burn, and both Hiroshi and Okami have a light bronze to their skin. I'll be the only one with miserable skin; even though I'm surrounded by Asians, a rarity for me on Earth, this is yet another reason I don't fit in here.

"Which way should we go?" Miki inquires, looking to Hiroshi for an answer.

Okami responds instead, "We need to go left." He steps to the left, but no one follows. "What are you doing? It's this way."

Hiroshi hesitates. "I thought the castle was toward the north."

"No, it's to the west. If you want to go on the wrong trail, then go for it, but I'm going west." Ignoring Hiroshi's concerns, he hikes down the trail to the left, giving us little choice but to follow him. The sun glares at us, off into the sunset isn't as romantic as people think, it's actually quite annoying and the bright light is giving me a headache.

The sun sinks lower and lower, Okami still proudly leads the way, but the rest of us exchange glances of doubt.

Miki tugs on Hiroshi hand, he clears is throat and voices our concerns. "Okami, where's the castle? It's going to be dark soon. Even with traveling as slow as we are, we should be there by now."

"If you think you're so smart, then we can ask someone for directions."

"Fine, we'll ask the first person we see."

"Wait a second." Miki pulls Hiroshi's fingers again. "We haven't seen anyone all day. What makes you think we will see someone now?"

Hiroshi replies calmly, "Don't worry, if we are where I think we are, then we'll be approaching people soon."

Stars pop out one by one in the sky above, the three moons shining bright. Torches flicker down the trail, there is a tall wooden archway, and two watchman posted on either side.

"Excuse me," Miki approaches one of the men. "We are lost. Could you give us directions on how to get to the castle?"

"And why would you need directions to the castle?" The guard folds his arms across his armored chest.

"Umm, we want to visit while we still can. Once the princess returns it will be off limits."

The other guard is more forthcoming, "You head back up this path and turn left at the fork in the road. It's the path heading north. It's only about an hour from there, but be careful. The castle has been abandoned for so many years, and there's no telling what you'll find there."

"Thank you." She bows and waves good-bye.

Miki returns to us and I ask, "Why did you talk to the villagers instead of Hiroshi?"

"Since I'm human, he nudged me to talk with them, it's less threatening, it being dark and all."

"I didn't even think about that."

Miki's countenance changes as she addresses Okami. "Okami," she states haughtily, savoring the moment. "They said we need to go back where we came from, and take the path that heads north."

He barks, "So I've heard."

75

The three moons shining above give us a glimmer of visibility as we back track to the fork in the road. Miki and I both drag our feet in fatigue. I miss riding in a car, I miss home, I miss Mom and Dad. Tears sting the corners of my eyes.

As if he can hear my thoughts, Hiroshi looks over his shoulder at me. His golden eyes reflect the moonlight, they are soft, full of sympathy.

Tilting my head downward, I shoot my hand up to my forehead to cover my face.

He slows his pace, allowing me to catch up with him. Placing his hand on my shoulder he whispers, "You're doing great. I promise we'll stop now."

Refusing to believe him, I don't dare look at him.

His hand slips of my shoulder, "It's too late to continue on. We will camp here for the night and get started in the morning."

Relief and guilt trickle down my spine, he was being honest. Could he really be different from other yokai? Even with his bloodlust?

Finally resting my head on the thin cotton pillow, I'm suddenly very aware of the trauma my body has been through. Every inch of my body pleads for a hot bath, if only I could comply. I've never been this active in my life, most of my time was spent studying, reading books. I thought walking before was bad enough, but now with Okami, I've entered a new level of torture.

Miki is sound asleep before she pulls the covers up. Hiroshi kneels down, and tucks her in. With each act of kindness, his true nature peaks through, but will it be enough to prevent him from committing homicide?

Again Hiroshi and Okami sleep on the opposite side of the crackling fire. The warm glow illuminates his golden hair, snug in his bedroll, his eyes shut. Why do I let my thoughts wander back to him? At times I sense a connection with him; my heart pounds hard, trying to send me a signal, whether it's telling me to run and hide, or to kiss him, I have no idea. Smashing these thoughts deep down, I gaze up at the countless number of twinkling stars, swirls of color smear across the sky, galaxies upon galaxies dot the blackness, could Earth be one of the twinkling lights above me?

8

"We're never going to find the castle," Miki whines, I don't blame her though, I feel exactly the same way. We had to wake up early to make up for time lost the previous day. I've never been a morning person, ever. Back home I was always running late to things because I would sleep in 'till the last possible minute. Another reason why I never did my hair or makeup.

Okami grunts, "It's up ahead, just wait and see."

"It wouldn't be the first time you've gotten us lost."

"Correction, if we get lost this time, it's your fault. You are the one who asked for directions, not me," he snarls.

We weren't walking but five more minutes when tall iron gates come into view, the dirt road gives way to a cobblestone path. "That must be the entrance to the castle," I say breathlessly.

"Of course it is. What else would it be?" Okami practically spat the words out. Jeez, that guy needs a chill pill, a really big one.

Following the stone path, the castle soon appears. The grand structure towers higher than any building in Nihon I've seen. As we get closer, the imperfections show through; weeds growing over the stone path, shutters falling off, shingles missing. I pause to take it all in.

"It's so big." Miki stares in amazement. "It's the biggest thing I've ever seen. It must have five levels!"

Although this castle isn't a skyscraper, it's still massive in size and was built with expert craftsmanship, unlike the small huts I've seen most of the villagers living in.

We carefully climb the grand steps, the boards creak under our weight. The castle's been abandoned, for some reason I expected there to be servants and staff, waiting for the princess to arrive. The two large doors leading inside have a giant cherry tree engraved upon them, the red hue of the wood is similar to that of Hiroshi's home.

"Go ahead, open it," Okami commands.

Hiroshi slowly reaches, but before he grasps the handle, Okami impatiently flings open both doors. He marches inside and is pummeled to the ground.

"The princess!" Hiroshi exclaims, eyes wide and claws extended.

There on the floor, a girl is wrestling with Okami. Her thin black and blue armor make her look like a ninja. Blue energy shoots from her hands. She's just like me! The girl controls the light into a rope and wraps it around her victim. Too busy with one opponent, she doesn't notice the other from behind.

Hiroshi grabs her shoulders and head, in ready position to break her neck. "Are you the princess?" He growls.

His voice send chills down my spine, he isn't the man I've come to know over the past few days.

In the same evil voice he roars, "Are you the princess?" The muscles in his arms and fingers flex. He's going to kill her!

His hands twitch, and she screams, "No! I'm not the princess!"

"How do I know you're not lying to me?" Hiroshi twists her head.

"I come from Maaku. At the age of three, we are branded. You will find the mark on my left wrist."

"Check her, Miki."

Miki drops my hand and scuttles over to examine her wrist. "She's telling the truth."

Reluctantly, Hiroshi opens his hands to free her. "Let me see your wrist." He snatches her hand and sees the mark for himself. "It's scarred over. You're telling the truth. What are you doing here? I almost killed you."

"I came here to protect the princess." She says bitterly through gritted teeth. The girl tries to yank her wrist away from Hiroshi, but he holds it firmly.

Her arm is now slightly twisted and from this new angle I have a clear view of her wrist. The mark is three circles, about the size of quarters, lined up leading from her wrist up her arm. The middle circle is slightly larger than the others, and the third is the smallest circle. There is also a small dot next to the third circle. They are the three moons in the sky; the dot must signify the star from the prophecy.

"Then she's here? Where is she?" Okami asks while struggling to stand, but he's still bound on the floor.

"The princess is not here. As I said, I'm waiting for her, and I will kill any demons who enter. I am loyal to the royal family."

"Let me go already?" Okami whines, desperately trying to wiggle out of her energy rope.

"I should kill you instead." She snaps.

Hiroshi releases the girl. "I could have killed you, but I spared your life. You should have the decency to do the same."

"Fine." She reluctantly reaches down and places her hand on the blue rope. It disintegrates without a trace of its existence.

"Thank you. Now, tell me where she is." Okami's voice is lighter than usual.

"I don't know, and even if I did, I wouldn't tell a demon, especially you. I'm going to wait here for her return, and if you know what's best for you, you'll leave."

"Ancestors," Okami curses, the words rolling off his tongue with a hiss. He stalks toward her, but Hiroshi steps in the way.

When I agreed to take this trip with them, I accepted I would be traveling with a yokai, but the two of them are more dangerous than I anticipated.

The girl cocks her head, "What are two human girls doing with these creeps?" She gives us a suspicious once-over. Her braided black hair is secured by a blue ribbon. The features of her face are stern and confident. She's older than I am, early twenties I think. "You're not their slaves, are you?"

"No," Miki squeaks. Not very reassuring.

"Then, you're their girlfriends? Disgusting. They are yokai, and you are so young."

"No, you don't understand." A tinge of anger is in her now bold speech. "I'm Miki, and Hiroshi is my brother. He saved me and the people of Unmei." Miki hugs Hiroshi.

Nodding to Okami. "What about him?"

"That's Okami. He's our friend."

"And you? What's your story?" Her bright blue eyes squint and her eyebrows draw together. Does she recognize me?

"I'm Rika, I've been traveling with them while working on my powers."

"You have powers?" The girl's eyes light up.

"Well, yes."

"What kind? Acrobatics, fighting, coercion, telekinesis? I've always wanted to meet someone who has mind control. There are so many gifts out there. Which did you receive?

"I can manipulate energy."

"That's amazing. Being able to control your essence as energy is one of the most rare and special gifts. What color is yours? Mine is blue as you saw."

"It's red."

Her jaw drops, but her lips remain pressed together. She takes a more casual tone, "Red, I'd love to see a demonstration."

Hiroshi steps uncomfortably close to the girl. Standing straight next to each other, she is only two or three inches shorter than him. Her build is not bulky, but she is strong and intimidating. "Now that you know so much about us, why don't you tell us more about yourself?"

"My name is Osamu. I come from Maaku. I have trained all of my life to protect the princess, and now I'm here awaiting her arrival. That's pretty much it."

"What's it like, training for combat?" Miki asks excitedly.

"It was my duty and honor to prepare myself for the important task of guarding the royal family. Maaku takes great pride in being the village chosen for raising warriors to be the army and guards of the royal palace."

"I've only heard stories. I didn't think that the people of Maaku still carried on that tradition. Why aren't there more soldiers?" Miki's eyes fill with longing; it's clear that her heart's desire is to be a warrior for the princess, just like Osamu.

"That's for another time. Enough about me. Rika, what are you able to do with your powers so far?"

83

"Um, that's the thing. I haven't really learned how to control it yet."

"What? You're kidding. You're in your late teens, and you can't wield the light?"

"I've only recently discovered my abilities."

Dumbfounded, she takes hold of my hand and pulls me further into the castle. "We've got work to do."

"Wait, where are we going?" I tug my hand away.

She lowers her voice to a harsh whisper, "It's imperative you learn to use your powers, and that's exactly what you're going to do. I will train you. If you are to be around these demons, you need to know how to defend yourself."

"Wait a second! What are we supposed to do?" Okami blocks our path.

"Get out of our way, wolf. You can leave and never return."

"Come on Hiroshi. Let's leave. She's not worth my time. We can look for the princess ourselves." He heads for the door.

"Hold on Okami, we can wait 'till tomorrow." Hiroshi walks after him.

"What, you'd pick this human over your lifelong friend! Every minute counts. While you're waiting here for her, someone else will be gaining the power of the princess." He bursts out the front doors. Good riddance.

"I'll go after him," Hiroshi calls out while rushing outside. Miki follows him, while Osamu drags me deeper into the castle. I hope she's the good guy, because I'm all alone with her now.

Eventually we come to an inner courtyard that steps down to a garden. The plants are overgrown, most shriveled up and brown. A pond in the middle is filled with a green sludge.

She whips around, her face inches from mine. "What on Nihon do you think you are doing with those creeps?"

"I've already told you, they are helping me practice my powers."

"Don't give me lies. Besides the fact you can't even summon them, I know who you are. Your true name is Ristuko, you are the princess." She kneels down on her left knee, her right hand rolls into a fist covering her heart, and she drops her head.

"Please don't do that. You have me mistaken for someone else."

Lifting her head she stands up. "You give me so little credit. The village of Maaku is dedicated to protecting the royal family. The ones who complete the most rigorous of training are sworn to secrecy and allowed into the caves of Mt. Naisho, there in the ancient scrolls it predicts that the princess is the only one who can manipulate red energy. Red is the essence of the royal lineage. You are the proper age, recently got your powers, and have the royal color. You are the princess. The thing I don't understand is why you are putting yourself at risk by hanging around those creatures. They want to kill you!"

The blood drains from my face and I have the inkling to faint. "No, no. I'm not even from here."

"That proves it. The princess was sent away during the rebellion."

I don't know what to believe anymore. First the crow, now this royal guard. "It's all circumstantial." I'm no one special. Hiroshi said it himself, I'm not powerful enough to be the legendary princess. It's preposterous.

"Say what you wish, but you're not safe around yokai, no matter who you are. They are the ones who started the rebellion. Thinking it was better for the yokai to rule Nihon than the humans."

"Why?"

"Power, control, why else?"

"What am I to do? Stay here with you?"

She rubs her forefinger and thumb on her chin. "No, it would be too suspicious. Even if it doesn't dawn on them right this minute, it's sure to hit them why you stayed and never came back."

"You took them down once, we could do it again."

She punches her hand into the palm of the other with a splash of blue light. "So I could, but then that little girl would hate you for killing her brother, and what if one of them escapes alive? The yokai would swarm us."

"Wait, I didn't say anything about killing them."

"How else are they to keep quite?" She shakes her head. "I will teach you how to use your powers. You may not like the idea of hurting anyone, but the time will come when you will have to destroy the yokai. It's your destiny. I pray you can rise to the occasion when that time comes. Let's get to work."

9

"I am focused!" I snap at Osamu. But I lied. How am I supposed to focus with all of her yelling?

"No, you're distracted. Go, you're done for the day."

"I'm not finished yet. I can't harness the light to appear, let alone do anything with it. I must show some sort of progress before we are through."

"Fine, then concentrate!" she yells, forming an energy beam whip. She swings and cracks it across my rear end.

"Ouch! That's it! I'm done with this foolishness. You're going to regret this!" My face burns with rage. I spin around to face her, but she's disappeared.

"Look at your hands." Instinctively I glance up toward the voice and see Osamu sitting on a tree branch. "Not at me, your hands."

Obeying I stare down at my hands. My hands are engulfed in red, the light dances on my hands like flames. "I've done it!"

"You're focused," she says with excitement.

"What do you mean? As soon as I stopped trying it worked."

"Exactly, you were concentrating on the wrong thing. When first learning to harness your abilities, it's easier when you are mad or in danger. Draw upon this feeling, make it work in your favor."

Miki bounces over to us with Hiroshi and Okami close behind. She jumps to the branch below Osamu and swings back and forth.

Osamu cocks her eyebrow, "Why didn't you mention you're gifted as well? You could've been training with us."

Miki releases the bark as if it was hot iron. Landing softly on the ground she scurries to the safety of Hiroshi's shadow.

Osamu leans against the tree trunk. "I didn't mean to frighten you young one."

"How did you know?" Hiroshi clenches his jaw.

"I've trained with several who have the ability of acrobatics. I take it you've been concealing her gift. I don't blame you. Many girls have been slaughtered as soon as there are suspicions. What's incredible is she would be protected by non-other than a yokai."

"How dare you insinuate I could hurt Miki."

Osamu glides off the tree and marches into his personal space. "You wish to harm the princess, why is she different?"

His muscles are tightening, his claws fanning out. Miki's still huddled behind him.

"Stop this." I shove myself between the two, they're so close I'm squeezed between them. My chest presses against his firm stomach. I feel him exhale slowly. "Let's go for a walk." I slip my fingers over his. A sliding sensation tingles my fingers as he retracts his talons .

Alarmingly he locks onto my hand and pulls me away. Adrenaline pumps through me. I follow him out of the courtyard, through hallways, and up a staircase. No one follows us.

At the end of a long and narrow hallway he drops my hand, I tumble to the ground. Immediately I see the look of regret on his face. Kneeling beside me, he brushes back a lock of hair laid across my face, "I'm so sorry." He rubs his forehead with his thumb and forefinger. Taking a much needed deep breath he sits crossed legged on the floor. "Thanks for stepping in back there. I normally don't let people get to me, but when it comes to Miki—"

"You don't have to explain."

He stares at me with those golden eyes and cracks a smile. The hallway is dark, save the small streams of light coming from the small dust covered window next to us. His head tilts and the next moment his lips are pressed against mine.

My eyelids instinctively slam shut, my heart flutters. He lifts away all too quickly, but I linger, half expecting another encounter. A few seconds pass buy and I flash my eyes open, he's gone. Where did he go? I stand up, my head dizzy. Leaning against the wooden paneling of the walls I smooth out my kimono. What was that all about?

It takes me ages to find my way back downstairs and into the inner courtyard. Osamu is sitting on a bench with a bowl of rice and vegetables. "Took you long enough."

"Me? What about you? You could've come looking for me and helped me through this maze of a castle."

She chuckles, "You're a big girl. Here, eat up." She hands me the wooden bowl and flat spoon. "And take this, Miki told me you don't have any nightwear." She places an off-white night shirt on my lap.

"Thank you." I whisper.

She slaps her large hands on her knees. "I'm off to bed. You're sleeping quarters are with Miki. Straight through these doors on the right."

I'm left alone to my own thoughts. I push the rice and bits of tubers around. Just when I think I've got a handle on things, everything turns upside down again. As I bring a scoop of food up to my lips, I flash back to the rapid kiss from Hiroshi. My first kiss ever. My heart beats hard in confusion. Was it fear or attraction I felt?

I toss and flop in my bedroll, unable to find a comfortable position. No matter what I do, each time I begin to drift off, I'm startled awake again. It doesn't make sense. I get out of bed before dawn, Miki's still snoring softly sprawled out in her bedroll with her toes peeking out from under the blankets.

My big toe bumps into a bundle of clothes outside my room with a note neatly placed on top, "Begin your practice in this." I unfold a blue pair of pants with a draw string, and a pull over shirt; similar to nurse's scrubs. The subtle weight of the pants on my hips is strange after wearing a kimono. The prospect of becoming better acquainted with the energy within me sends a thrill up and down my spine. I head to the inner courtyard with a bounce in my step.

Osamu is sitting next to the slime green pond, her legs folded across each other with the bottoms of her bare feet facing upward. Her eyes are closed, her hands placed near her belly button in the shape of a triangle. A soft blue glow hovers in her palms. She opens one eye, "Couldn't sleep?"

I shake my head.

"Good, it's time to learn." She pops up and quickly strides next to me. Straight to the point as always. "Engage your powers, then bring your hand toward your chest. Make sure it's flat, and with a flicking motion, reach your hand out in front of you."

I focus on the time my powers first appeared, when the crow demon lifted me into the air and I thought I would surely die. A twinge of fear passes through me, down to my hands, activating the energy within me. Next I follow her instructions, but the red light goes nowhere.

She grabs my arm from behind. "Keep your hand flat, and then you fling your arm forward." Shards of the red light fly into a rotted log..

"Woah, it's as if I threw daggers."

"I call it energy daggers for that very reason." She twirls her finger, instructing me to repeat the drill. Osamu and I practice for several hours nonstop. The old log has been split so many times, it's nearly disintegrated. I enjoy working with her, but toward the end I'm getting pretty fed up with her. She's like a drill sergeant; the training tactics are effective, but harsh and annoying.

"I washed your kimono for you." Miki holds up the freshly cleaned garment.

"Thank you, after the tunnels in Heiwa it needed it."

"Take a bath before you change clothes. There is a river near here and hot springs. I need one too. Would you like to come with us Miki?" Osamu cracks her neck from side to side.

"You bet I would." Miki hustles inside the castle. Osamu and I casually follow.

"Where are you guys going?" Hiroshi asks.

"To the nearby hot springs," I answer.

"Can we come?" Hiroshi asks.

Okami huffs and rolls his eyes.

I blush and my breath catches, he acts as if nothing happened between us. "I don't see why not. Of course you'll have to bathe and relax in separate areas than us." As soon the words pass my lips, Osamu glares at me and sighs. I guess she didn't want them to come.

Washing in the river is a chilling experience, but the hot springs are a different story. The heat is soothing to both mental and physical aches. I enjoy the peace as long as possible, reluctantly leaving when Osamu suggests we head back. We meet up with the guys outside the castle.

Hiroshi lounges on the steps, while Okami paces back and forth with his hands behind his back. "Finally, you're back. You girls take forever to do anything. Especially you Rika." He spins on his heels to face me. "I had hoped your delay was due to a yokai gobbling you up, but alas, fate is not that kind to me."

Hiroshi stiffens and opens his mouth to defend me, but I cut him off, "I am in no mood for your whining. I had an amazing time, and I'm not going to let you rain on my parade." I purposefully bump into his arm with my shoulder as I pass by.

He and the others follow me inside. "That is beside the point. We must leave."

Osamu, irritated by his ill manners, throws her hands in the air. "And where do you plan on going? I was your big lead."

"Anywhere is better than here," he mutters. "But if you must know, the seer in Mirai."

"Like he would help you?" She mocks.

"He'd better," Okami says acidly.

"I think it's best we're off now. Thank you for the accommodations," Hiroshi says politely while giving a slight bow.

93

"Thank you Osamu," I say a bit gloomily. There's no telling the amount of danger I'll be walking into when I leave this place.

We pack up our things and head south, leaving Osamu and the castle behind.

10

Calls and whistles from various birds echo through the serenity of the forest, until Okami's complaining begins. "The seer better be obliging–" He cracks the knuckles in both his hands and neck, emphasizing the threat.

Before an argument can start I ask, "How far away is Mirai?"

Hiroshi eagerly answers, "It's pretty close to our village, Unmei. It will take us a few days to get there."

"At last we'll be close to home," Miki chirps, but her face turns somber. "We've been away for a while now." She looks down at the ground, her voice void of the excitement that had been there only moments ago. "I've never been away from home this long before."

Glancing over at the small girl, she wrings her hands nervously. Homesick, I know the feeling. I miss the familiarity of my house, my friends, Mom and Dad. Even with the lies about my heritage, Dad's cheating, and Mom's neglect. Maybe my absence is good for them, it will give them the space they wanted. When I get back, everything will be sorted out, for better or worse. I wrap my arm around her in an attempt to comfort her and myself.

We travel hard and fast for several days, time passes quickly since we engage in conversation the entire way. Each day I get stronger and the hiking becomes less intense, my body is adjusting to this new lifestyle. My kimono fits a little looser, finally losing that last ten pounds, not the way I expected to. And the icing on top of the cake? For once everyone gets along.

Night falls, and Hiroshi asks, "How tired is everyone?"

"I'm fine," I answer while stretching my calves.

"Same here, why?" Miki asks while switching her bag to the opposite shoulder.

"Because we are getting close to Mirai, and if you guys are up for it, we could get there tonight."

"Let's do it," I answer.

"Me too." Miki cartwheels around me, then Hiroshi.

"At last we will get decent ground covered," Okami had to put in his snide remark.

"Then it's settled. Once we get there, we can rent a room at an inn."

"Really?" Miki shrieks and grabs onto my arm.

"Yes really." Hiroshi laughs.

Not twenty minutes later, exhaustion creeps in. My enthusiasm is gone, and my feet are aching. I should have quit when I was ahead. "I'm spent. Let's camp on the road."

"Don't worry Rika, you won't regret it. We are going to stay at an inn. I've heard they have the softest beds," Miki tries to reassure me.

I don't know how she can have so much energy. I wish my own abilities helped more in the stamina department. It creates a new appreciation for exercising; if I hadn't been so lazy at home, this wouldn't be so hard.

If Mrs. Takara hadn't sent me here I would be living with Grandma and Grandpa . Maybe even starting my summer psychology program soon. My nights would be filled with studying and Grandma's warm peanut butter cookies.

If I ever do return to Earth, would Willamette University accept me back, or would they brand me a flake? I've always been a straight A student, never skipping school, consistently getting to class on time every day. They'd have to accept me, wouldn't they?

Deep in thought Miki interrupts me, "We're here! We're here!" She circles us cheering.

I couldn't be happier to see village gates. The town is dark except the torches posted at either side of the entrance.

Hiroshi stops in front of the first building we see. "Here we are." He smiles triumphantly. One could hardly extrapolate this was a place for people to sleep. The roof is moss covered, the window shutters hang by their rusted hinges. This place is a mess. Can this really be the place we've worked so hard to get to?

We step inside, and I can't believe my eyes. The room is bright and cheerful; there is a bear rug on the floor and a fire burning in the brick fireplace in the corner. Four half drunken men sitting at the bar, cheerfully sing a drinking song while clanging their foaming wooden chalices together, spilling the amber liquid onto the wooden planks below their stools.

The smell of roasting meat makes my mouth water. Now I can see what Miki was talking about. Of course this is nothing compared to the Four Seasons Hotel back home, but this is a different building compared to the shambles I saw outside.

At the front desk Hiroshi speaks with the innkeeper. "We would like a room please."

The man strums his fingers on the countertop. "And who are you? Two demons coming into my establishment with women, and wanting to spend the night?"

"I'm Hiroshi the protector of Unmei, and who are you to question my honor?"

The man scrambles to bow, "Please forgive me, I have heard of your dedication to the people of Unmei. However, I do expect full payment in the morning."

"Of course," he replies.

"Right this way." The innkeeper leads us down the hall to our room.

"I will give you payment first thing in the morning," Hiroshi reassures the innkeeper. "What time is check out?"

"Don't worry about it. Sleep in. You are getting here late as it is. Might as well get your money's worth."

"Thank you." Hiroshi bows, and we all enter into the room.

"This is great!" Miki runs over to a shelf which has the bedrolls stored on it. She grabs two and lays them on the floor. "Rika, come here and feel yours."

I rub the silky fabric between my fingers. "You're right, this is the softest bed I've ever felt." Still, I'd rather have my memory foam mattress back home.

"I knew you'd love it." She roles out her bed and mine.

Miki and I change into our sleepwear behind dressing screens. We get ready for bed and are in our bedrolls within a few minutes. We say our good nights and lay down to sleep.

I close my eyes, and while falling asleep Miki whispers to me, "Rika, are you awake?"

I don't want to admit it, but I roll over anyway. "I am now. What do you need?"

"Do you like Hiroshi? I mean, do you think he's cute?"

Taken aback a little, I'm not sure how to respond. "Shhh, how can you ask such a question when he's right over there."

"Don't worry, he's sleeping."

Listening carefully, I barely make out the heavy breathing of the men on the other side of the room. "Only if you answer my question first."

"Sure, ask me anything."

"Why didn't you tell me about your powers?"

The hard gulp she takes is audible, "I've known I was different my entire life. My parents discouraged me from playing with other kids, or being around others in general.

"They thought people would be afraid of me, and I would be a magnet for the yokai. I was only five when Hiroshi saved our village, he was the only one I felt comfortable telling my secret too. He understood the gravity of the situation, and we've done our best to keep my condition hidden. Now that you and Okami know, it's not something I can keep secret anymore." She pauses, "enough about me, tell me about you and Hiroshi," she giggles.

"Well, just between you and me, I think he is incredibly cute, but you can't tell anyone." If he finds out I'll die of embarrassment.

"I promise I won't. Good night."

"Good night." I try to rest my aching body, but the wheels are ever turning in my mind. He's a yokai, with the purpose of murder and conquest. Besides, he's too good looking to take much of an interest in me, just like Brandon.

I wonder what Brandon's doing back home. Does he realize I'm gone? I doubt he would unless I'm on the back of a milk carton, and even then it's negligible. Still, I miss him. I miss his hair, the way he smiles so sweetly when he laughs. I miss my friends, my teachers, but most of all Missy.

The next morning we all oversleep; I awake to beams of light streaming through our window. "What a perfect way to start the day," I say, sitting up in my bed and stretching my arms into the air.

"You've said it," Miki lazily yawns and stretches her arms as well.

"Did everyone else sleep well?" I ask as I get out of bed.

"Yes." Hiroshi props up on his elbows in bed. Okami growls and rolls over.

Two dressing screens are tucked in the corner. Miki and I dress behind them, while the guys put the beds away. Ready to leave, we walk down the hall back to the check-in desk.

The innkeeper welcomes us with a burly smile. "Good morning. I hope you've enjoyed your stay."

"Yes, thank you." Hiroshi reaches into his bag and pulls out a coin satchel. He withdraws three coins for the innkeeper.

The innkeeper counts and places them in a drawer in his desk. "We have leftovers from breakfast. Would you like some?"

"We sure would." Miki runs up to the desk. The innkeeper leaves the room for a few minutes, and then returns with a wooden crate of food. "Thank you so much." Miki says, as she takes the crate.

"You are welcome young one. May the ancestors bless your journey, and thank you for your service." He bows down to Hiroshi, and Hiroshi bows as well. The friendly innkeeper waves good-bye as we leave.

"That was so nice of him." Miki hugs the food crate.

Hiroshi slows his pace, looking for a good place to sit down. He soon points to a tree just off the path. "Over there's a nice spot."

The grass is plush and perfect. Miki reluctantly gives the food box to Hiroshi, and he divvies out the food.

With our bellies full, we rise to leave, but a thin man in long brown robes approaches us.

Excitedly Hiroshi bows, "are you the seer?"

"No, no, only his assistant." He rubs the side of his bald head nervously.

"When is he going to get here?" Okami demands.

The man widens his eyes as he regards Okami's fangs, his voice trembles, "He comes when he is needed."

Okami advances, "you'd better get him, now!"

Hiroshi wedges himself between Okami and the seer's assistant. "Thank you for your help." He glares at Okami.

"You are most welcome," the man bows and rushes away.

"Why do you always have to be so rude?" Miki plops down with her arms folded. Okami ignores her and rests himself on the other side of the tree. Miki looks at Hiroshi, her eyes full of fire.

"I know, I know, he can be kind of a jerk, don't worry. It'll be fine." Hiroshi sits down next to Miki and puts his arm around her.

Miki lowers her voice and whispers. "Just between us, I don't like him." I feel the same way.

We sit in silence for a while, until Miki starts to fidget and becomes restless. "I wonder what the seer looks like?"

"Like a person, what else would he look like?" Okami smirks. "And no, I'm not being rude Miki, I'm just stating the obvious."

I wish I had the courage to stand up to him more. There are so many things I'd like to say to him. Deep breaths, in and out. I can't let myself get so worked up, I might say something I'll regret. With tensions high, we all try to keep our mouths shut and wait for the seer.

An hour or so has passed, and now Okami's irritation is evident. "Where is that man?" He begins pacing. "Who does he think he is? Making us wait around all day."

"Hold on, he will be here soon enough." Hiroshi shrugs his shoulders.

Okami halts. "I'm going to go find him." He whips around and almost runs into someone.

"Who are you going to find?" a dusty voice asks. We all turn to look. Standing in front of Okami is an elderly man, his face full of wrinkles, with no hair to speak of except for his bushy gray eyebrows. He's dressed in a brown robe with rope sash, simple but dignified.

"If you must know old man, we are waiting for the seer. We've been waiting for hours."

He raises his hand to push the old man out of his way, but the old man speaks again, "With an attitude like that, you will never find him." The old man smiles and slowly turns to walk away.

"Wait!" I stand up frantically, almost tripping over myself in my haste. "You're the seer, aren't you?" Instead of waiting for an answer, I just bow, almost out of instinct.

"I'm glad to see that you are not as blind as your friend." The old man bows in return. "What can I do for you?"

Hiroshi rushes to his feet and bows. "We are searching for the princess."

"Ah, what a selfish aspiration." The seer shuffles closer to us.

Hiroshi tenses, balling his hands into fists. "You are too quick to judge. I'm going to use her powers to help others."

"If you were truly selfless, you would spend your time helping her save this world, not trying to steal her power so *you* can save it." He glances over to me and then back to Hiroshi.

"She hasn't done anything for this world." As his fists clench tighter, his knuckles turn white. He elevates his voice. "She has wasted her gift. She has sat idle. She's a coward, useless. Our world is heading for destruction. I can't keep waiting for her to suddenly show up and care."

The seer cocks an eyebrow, "The princess only recently came of age. You expected a child to fight to the death, yet you're overprotective of your own?"

"We didn't wait here for hours to hear your babbling old man. Tell us where the princess is!" Okami's eyes flicker with rage, the anger welling within him on the brink of overflowing.

"Calm down," his raspy voice commands. "If you must know where she is, or rather where she will be, return to your home, Unmei." His bushy brows raise, revealing his pale brown eyes. "You'd better rethink your intentions. The power you hope to achieve by killing the princess will never match the strength that the two of you working together will have." After saying this, the seer sets his eyes on me. "One more thing. You," he points with his finger covered in liver spots, "come here."

Does he know something he shouldn't? Why does he want to talk to me? Walking away he motions with his hand for me to follow him. I hurry to catch up.

Once we had created some space between us and the others, he turns to face me, "Don't look so worried." He cracks a smile to relieve the tension. The wrinkles of his face pile on top of one another, covering where each one ends and the next begins. "I don't bite. Let's take a walk."

"All right." I smile, relieved that this man seems friendly enough. We stroll down a path at the edge of the village.

We pass by golden wild flowers on either side of the path, bees buzz between the blossoms. Once clear from the sight of the others, the seer begins again with the sharpness of a freshly sharpened sword, "What are you doing, traveling with yokai?"

"They are my friends."

"They are a mercenaries. The ransom villages pay to keep yokai from murdering them in inexcusable. And they claim they are the villages "protectors". It's deplorable. The only one in that group that would not kill you is the little girl, and you know it."

"What else should I do?"

"If you flee it will arise suspicion, they will hunt you down and find you. They know your scent. By staying with them your life is also in jeopardy. You must be careful, persuade them to see the princess in a different light."

"Why?"

"It is your destiny." The old man pats my shoulder and leaves.

"Wait, what is that supposed to mean?" I call out for an answer, but the seer continues on as if I'm not even here. My destiny? I rub the bridge of my nose toward my forehead and inhale. Why is everyone so obsessed with the princess, can't they nominate a president?

"What did he say?" Hiroshi asks impatiently, as I rejoin the group.

"Um, he told me to stop traveling with yokai." Total lie.

"How dare he!" Hiroshi takes a large stride in the direction we last saw the seer.

"Wait!" I reach for his arm but miss and yank his tale.

He yelps.

"Sorry, Hiroshi. Forget about him, he wanted to make sure I wasn't a prisoner or something. He doesn't think it's proper for a girl my age to be left alone with you two. It's nothing personal."

His face droops, his energy drained. "This trip was a waste of time." He leans against the tall maple tree. "Are you sure he didn't say anything else?" His eyes twinkle in the hopes that I had forgotten some crucial detail.

"No, nothing else. I'm sorry."

Hiroshi's eyes dim, "All this work to be told to go home."

I sense someone looking at me, I snap around, Okami is staring at me. His piercing hatred is almost tangible. He knows something, or at the very least suspects something's up. Perhaps Mrs. Takara will be in Unmei when we get back, that's at least something to look forward to.

Hiroshi pushes away from the tree. "Let's go." He picks up his bag, and we follow the path that leads out of the village.

"This is a good move for us." Miki tries to lighten the mood. "At least we know where the princess will be."

Hiroshi's eye light up once again. "You're right. Going home isn't admitting defeat, it's the completion of this chapter in our search. We just have to wait for the princess to come to us."

As we pass through the village gates, a frantic voice calls out, "Wait, wait!"

Someone is chasing after us. As he gets closer, I can barely make out who it is; it's the man who told us about the seer earlier.

"I'm so glad I found you before you left." Placing his hands on his knees he takes deep breathes, between gasps for air he says, "The seer just had a vision. Your village is in danger. If you don't hurry back it will be destroyed."

11

With the man's urgent message still ringing in my ears, Hiroshi takes hold of my hands. "We have to hurry. I will carry you, and Okami, you carry Miki." He swings around in an attempt to lift me onto his back, but my kimono makes it awkward. The bottom is narrow and doesn't allow my legs to separate enough to wrap around him.

This will be a long trip, I can't kneel on his back the entire way. I attempt to widen the bottom of the kimono by stretching it with my legs, but no luck. This is so embarrassing.

Hiroshi sighs in frustration. "You'll have to loosen that kimono to sit properly." Scratch that last thought, *this* is embarrassing. At least Hiroshi is the one holding me, and not Okami. My face burns hot as I try to loosen my kimono without it falling off; Miki and Okami watch impatiently.

"Well, come on!" Okami shouts at me.

My hands fumble but my fingers manage to slip through the knot, loosening my obi. Without warning, he picks me up, and we're off. I didn't have a chance to retighten things, and the jostling has caused my obi to come undone.

The wind caused by Hiroshi' speed whips at my clothes, lifting it off my skin. Help, oh no. What should I do? Plan A, try to secure my clothes and possibly fall, or plan B, risk everything flying off?

A cool breeze blows across my stomach. Plan A! I let go of his shoulders for only a second, but the next thing I know I'm lying on the ground. I open my eyes to see everyone hovering around me.

"Are you hurt?" Miki leans over and brushes my hair away from my face.

"You're supposed to hold on ding bat," Okami rolls his eyes before yanking me to my feet.

"Be careful." Hiroshi pulls me away from Okami and holds me close to his chest. "Are you injured? You hit the ground pretty hard."

"Umm, no, I'm fine." I put my hand to back of my head, feeling the lump that's already forming.

"Let's get going then. We can't waste any more time. Are you ready?"

I re-tie the obi of my kimono and Hiroshi lifts me onto his back. I grip his shoulders tightly and pray we will get there in time to save the village. My mistake could cost people their lives.

Before the village comes into view, we hear screams piercing the forest. I feel Hiroshi's muscle ripple under my fingers. He sets off into a sprint. I can't believe he has the stamina to go on.

"Someone help me!" a woman screams and runs through the village gates. She doesn't get far before a bear yokai snatches her leg. His sharp claws dig into her foot as he pulls her back into the village.

"Let her go!" Hiroshi yells.

The bear picks her up and scampers into the forest. "Help me!" she cries out in desperation as they disappear into the trees.

"I'm going after her. You three check the village for demons." Hiroshi tosses me off his back.

"Wait," I protest, "I can help. Take me with you." I start to climb onto his back.

"Fine." In hot pursuit, we stumble upon the bear yokai and the woman within a few moments. He must think we're stupid or don't care since he's only a few paces from the edge of the forest. "Get away from her," Hiroshi demands.

The bear lifts his huge paw to maul the woman, ignoring Hiroshi and me. His hands, feet, and face are covered in brown mated fur. His head is shaped like a bear, but with no fur. I've noticed that some yokai look more like humans, while others more like animals. This one's definitely on the animal side.

If Hiroshi uses his agility and I use my powers, perhaps between the two of us we can stop him in time. I engage my powers, causing my hands to become engulfed in the red light, but Hiroshi throws me from him. "What are you doing?" I stumble on some twigs, but catch myself before I topple over.

He charges toward the bear. "Get away from her!" Hiroshi punches the yokai. He falls to the ground, eyes wide and stunned.

The bear slowly lifts his head. "What do you think you are doing? You have your own human to kill. Let me have mine." The bear stands up, completely dismissing Hiroshi yet again. He's acting like we're just being rude.

"Get out of here, or I will kill *you*!" Hiroshi roars at the bear demon.

"I can't believe it, a fellow yokai wanting to save humans. It's a pity what this world is coming to." The bear demon rises to his hind legs and lets a roar that vibrates my lungs. He snorts before dropping to all fours and charging.

Hiroshi lunges out of the way, but now I'm in line to get pummeled. I throw my hands in front of me, the red light still blazing.

The bear rears up in horror and excitement. "Killing you is worth more than every pathetic human in this village."

Hiroshi uses his razor sharp claws to lacerate the bear's back. The bear yokai gives a loud grunt and lumbers around to face his attacker. Hiroshi makes an X with his hands and uncrosses them fiercely, releasing his final blow on the bear by essentially ripping his face off. Blood splatters across Hiroshi's chest and face, his eyes briefly match the spray of color. He wipes the droplets from his cheeks and forehead.

The girl scrambles to her feet and rushes to Hiroshi. "Thank you for saving me." The girl throws her arms around his neck and gives him a long, passionate kiss.

I stand there stunned, seriously? Tears well up in my eyes. I should have known it was too good to be true, that someone could like me that way. For all I know, she's his girlfriend.

I dash out of there, taking me only a minute to enter town. My heart pounds as if I ran a marathon. Keep yourself together. If Okami knows you've been crying, he will just make fun of you. I take a deep, wavering breath to collect myself and wipe away my tears. After I compose myself, I find Miki helping an elderly woman to her feet.

"Could you help me get her inside?"

"Sure, no problem." My voices shakes despite my efforts. I put my shoulder under one of the elderly woman's arms. I could handle her weight without a problem normally, but with all these emotions coursing through me, I'm barely able to lift her.

Miki wraps her arm around her waist. "What's wrong Rika?"

"Nothing." I hide my face behind the old woman. We help her up the road and into her hut. Gradually we lower her down onto her bed.

"Thank you so much. When that bear demon came through, he knocked me over and kept going. I'm so glad you came along." The old woman is addressing Miki, but she gestures her thumb at me like a hitchhiker. "I know what's wrong with her: boys. It's always men at that age." She rolls over to me. "Don't worry dear, if he's not the one, there'll be plenty of others."

113

I consider lying and brushing it off, but I decide to tell the truth instead. "How did you know?"

"Lucky guess." She winks and her crow's feet deepen.

"Well now, there are plenty of other people who need help. I will be fine. You two run along."

We both stand and nod. "Good-bye," we call out as we exit the hut.

"Was the old woman right? Did Hiroshi do something?" Miki asks intently.

I stare at the pebbly ground and remain still for a moment. "Well, you see, the woman we rescued from the bear…when she was free, she kissed him." I shift my weight back and forth between my feet. "It's not like we are dating or anything. He's not obligated to me."

"I can't believe him. All this time, I thought he liked you. He always catches a glimpse of you when he thinks no one else is looking. Why would he do this? He's going to get it when I see him." Miki clenches her fists, upset that her plans to put us together are failing.

I put my feelings aside while we help villagers, before meeting up with Okami later in the day.

"I hope you two have been productive. Where's Hiroshi?" Okami doesn't greet us with a 'hello' he cuts to the point and demands to know what we've been doing. So typical.

"You don't want to know." Miki avoids the question and asks one of her own. "Are there any more yokai in town?"

He points his nose in the air and sniffs in several directions. "No, I can't smell any more, but there are plenty hanging around the outskirts."

"It's a good thing we came back when we did. This place is getting torn to pieces." Miki looks at the huts next to us. There are slashes through the roofs, door flaps missing.

"What's the matter with you?" Okami stares at me with a critical eye.

"Nothing," I answer, walking away. Jeez, people back home always wanted to know my personal life, and it's no different here.

"Wait, there is definitely something wrong with you. You look as if your favorite pet died. This doesn't have to do with Hiroshi, does it?" I hesitate, wondering if he could really care about my feelings.

He grabs my shoulder with the pads of his fingers and spins me around to face him. "It does. Seriously? What has he done? Walked off with some woman, I suppose. I bet she was prettier than you. It's not hard really."

Miki punches his arm. "Quit it, you're only making things worse."

"I can't believe you like him. He's yokai and you're human. Why would he even want to be with a human anyway? They are weak and pathetic."

"He was kissing a human, so just shut up!" I jerk away and run for home as fast as I can. I wish I could go to my real home. I would call Missy and tell her what's happening. She'd know what to say.

"Rika, wait!" Miki follows after me. "I will talk with him," she calls out. I reluctantly stop and let her catch up.

"That would only make things worse. If he wants to be with her, let him."

Miki trails close behind me back to our hut without pressing the issue further. As we get closer, I can tell that things have been crumbling at home as well. The once quaint little home is in shambles. Most of the windows are broken, the roof has multiple holes, and the door flap hangs only by a corner. The seer wasn't kidding when he said this village was nearing destruction. I'm glad we returned before there was nothing left to return to.

The married couple we had left to take care of the home come outside to greet us. They're smiling, but the dark circles around their eyes and hallowed out cheek bones tell the real story. They look like they've aged ten years. "We are so glad you are back," the woman exclaims as she hugs Miki.

"Me too." Miki grips her tightly.

"Me three," I shyly wave.

"You must be hungry. You've been gone a while. Why don't you come inside and tell me all about your adventures while I get dinner going. Where is Hiroshi?"

My heart thumps hard. Why do I care so much? This is so stupid.

"He and Okami are patrolling for demons." Miki answers.

"Who is Okami?" She asks.

"Oh, you haven't met Okami yet, he's one of Hiroshi's yokai friends. He's been traveling with us." Miki changes the subject, and we step inside. The outside is dilapidated, but at least it's still nice on the inside. A pitchfork and scythe lay next to the doorway. Are those just for farming, or was that their only means of defense?

I gaze over at the married couple chatting away with Miki, and I realize, I have no clue as to what their names are.

Either I take action and include myself in the conversation, or I wait here in the corner until someone realizes I'm here. Normally I would choose the later, but I can't be that melancholy if I'm to hold my own here. I promptly decide to introduce myself. I go over to the woman. "Um, excuse me."

"Yes, is there something I can get for you?"

"I'm fine. You see, I was just thinking that we haven't been properly introduced. I have no idea what your names are."

"Really? Huh, I guess you're right. I know your name is Rika. My name is Miyu, and this is my husband Kenta."

"Hello Rika." The young, suntanned man waves to me.

"Miyu and Kenta, nice to finally get acquainted with you."

"Well, how did you like the trip?" Miyu pats the seat next to her, and I sit down.

"It was great. I learned how to control my powers a lot better. I still need to practice more, but I've really improved."

"That's amazing. It seems to be rarity these days for humans to have powers." Miyu stands to stir a large pot on the cook stove. Maybe I shouldn't be telling everyone about my abilities.

"Are we having soup for dinner?" Miki asks.

"Yes we are. It will be ready in a little while." Miyu and Miki continue to chat, and I put in a comment here and there, but I don't say much. So engrossed in my own thoughts, when I finally take a look around, Kenta is missing. He must have gone outside without me noticing.

"It smells like dinner is almost ready." Miki's eyes light up.

"You sure like your food," Miyu kids.

"Yes, I do." She smiles proudly.

"You're in luck because dinner is done."

"Yippee! I will set the table." Miki runs over to the cupboard and pulls out the dishes.

"We're back," Hiroshi declares as he and Okami emerge through the doorway. My hearts leaps to my throat, my attempts to smother my feelings aren't going as planned. Did Okami tell him about our conversation earlier? I nervously look away before he can flash me one if his dashing grins, I don't think I could handle it.

"I wondered if you two were ever going to show up." Miyu gives Hiroshi a hug. "This must be Okami. It's nice to meet you. Miki has told me lots about you. Dinner is ready, could you call for Kenta?"

"Sure thing." Hiroshi leaves and returns with Kenta only moments later.

"That was fast." Miyu scrunches her eyebrows suspiciously.

"I could smell your delicious cooking out in the fields. I was almost home when Hiroshi stepped outside." Kenta gives Miyu a kiss. "Let's eat."

"How's the planting going?" Miyu sits down at the table.

"Not well dear. If we can't sow the eastern field by the end of the week there won't be enough food to last through the cold season. The yokai destroyed so many crops." Kenta and Miyu share a concerned frown.

We sit down to our meal, and everyone enjoys relaying the events of the past two weeks, except for me. Everyone else is having a good time, and all I can do is sit here and feel sorry for myself. It's as if no one will ever really like me. The only true friend I had back home was Missy. Sure there was Brandon, he was nice to me and all, but it's not like he chose to hang out with me. This new world is losing its charm. Will I ever get to go home, back to the people I know? My stomach churns nervously.

"Are you feeling well?" Hiroshi turns his attention to me. No one else notices that he's asked.

"I'm fine, really." I avert my gaze, I can't bear to make eye contact.

"You seem upset. You've barely touched your food. I'm sorry we couldn't stay longer at Osamu's. We can work on your training here though."

"Yeah, sure." I struggle to give a reassuring smile.

Satisfied with my answer, he nudges Okami's side and tells a joke.

I hold out for another half an hour before getting ready for bed. I slip under the covers while everyone else is still gossiping around the table.

"Are you sleepy already?" Miyu asks.

"Yes." I pretend to yawn. "It was a tiresome trip."

"All right. Good night then."

"Good night Rika," everyone else pipes in. I lay facing away from the crowd, eyes closed, pretending to sleep, but to no avail. Did the kiss in the castle mean anything to him? A little trail of tears run across the bridge of my nose and drop onto the blanket.

Time passes, and I hear Miki scolding Hiroshi. "You are an idiot. What were you thinking?"

"What are you talking about?"

"I mean why were you kissing that girl you saved from the bear demon?"

"I don't know. She kissed me after I saved her, that's all. I didn't even like it."

"I've been told otherwise. You're so dense, don't you know you hurt Rika's feelings? She was standing right there, and you kissed another girl. I told you that she likes you, and you went and blew it."

"She's overreacting, it didn't mean anything."

"Um, take it from me, she's probably right." It sounds as if Kenta has put his two cents in.

"Alright, I'll fix things later, but she's sleeping right now, and we all know how she likes her sleep."

"I don't think she will mind if you wake her up. Go talk to her," Miki pleads with him.

The group goes quiet, and I hear rustling from the table. The hairs on the back of my neck stand as I realize he's coming to over to me. Miki, why did you say anything? You promised!

He bends down, and while gently placing his hand on my arm, he whispers, "Rika, are you asleep?"

I flutter my eyes open and roll over to face him, not knowing what to expect. With a yawn I say, "I'm up now, is there something I can do for you?"

"I'm sorry to disturb you, but I need to speak with you."

"In here?" I peer around him to see Miki and Miyu staring at us.

"No, outside." We stand up, and I slide on my shoes. He hands me a wool blanket as we step outside. The air is cool, but not uncomfortable. I wrap the blanket around my shoulders, the fibers are scratchy against my neck.

We stroll down the dirt road a little ways before he continues the conversation. "Miki told me why you are upset. I didn't think you saw what happened."

"Would it have made a difference?"

"Yes, that woman means nothing to me. When she kissed me, all I could think about was securing the village."

"And what were you thinking about when you kissed me in the castle?" Why did I just say that? "I'm sorry, I shouldn't have asked," I stammer, fumbling to find the right words. "It's really none of my business." I turn to leave, but he swiftly grasps my forearm to stop me.

He tugs me around so he can see my face. "I was thinking about how lucky I am you fell into my arms." He steps closer, his face calm, his golden cat eyes gaze down at me. He leans in, I close my eyes, bracing myself. His muscular arms wrap around me, and he pulls me against his chest. "I'm sorry I made you cry."

I stand there frozen for a moment, not sure what to make of it. His long coarse hair tickles my cheeks. In his arms, I have an overwhelming sense of security. I know I shouldn't let myself become attached to him, but I can't help it. I think I'm falling for him.

"I should get you back to bed. It's getting cold out here." He relaxes his arms and backs away.

"Yeah, it is a bit chilly."

He places his left arm around me, his hand resting on my waist. My heart skips a beat, this is more than friendship. As we approach the hut, Miyu and Miki quickly dive inside. "I can't believe those two."

"I can." Hiroshi chuckles. We enter to see them calmly sitting at the table, as if nothing had happened.

"How was your walk?" Miki nonchalantly inquires. Hiroshi and I don't answer.

He escorts me to my bedroll. "Good night."

"Good night." I look up at his perfect face; he smiles and kisses me ever so lightly on the cheek.

Everything is whirling around in my head. The events replay over and over throughout the night.

12

My days have been uneventful, I help Miki with morning chores then practice sparring with Hiroshi and Miki. Hiroshi flashes an occasional wink, but nothing dramatic. Okami watches from the sidelines, claims he's perfect, doesn't need training. So far today has followed suit.

"I'm bored." Miki whines and drags her bare feet to the middle of the grassy area we use for sparring. She lazily preforms a tuck to shoot handstand. "Let's go to the orchard and collect petals."

"That's ridiculous. If we're going anywhere it's to teach the seer a lesson in honesty. How dare he lie to us about the princess, and now we have no leads." Okami throws a rock off into the horizon.

Hiroshi replies, "We haven't hunted in a few days and the meat supply is low. We can deal with the seer another time."

Miki dismounts from her handstand to an arabesque pose. "You two have fun, I know we will." She snatches my hand and we run off giggling.

I look back, Hiroshi waves with the tips of his fingers before following Okami off in the opposite direction.

We dash toward the waves of pink, my heart racing for joy instead of fear. Miki is my dearest friend on Nihon. Her long hair whips freely behind her. She flashes me a smile. This is the happiest I've been in my life. I wish there was a way to capture this moment and live here. To stay young, free, frolicking off with my friend, but I know there's more to life.

Petals rain down on us as we enter the orchard. She drops my hand and shoves me. "Tag, you're it." She darts around the trees.

"Hey, not fair!" I race after her. Her blush kimono blends in with the curtain of petals. I zig zag through the rows. "I'll get you back!" I sprint in an effort to overtake her. My breathing is heavy and I'm no longer able to see her. "Miki?" My feet scuff against the packed dirt to slow down. "Miki, where are you?"

A ball of light explodes next to me, dissipating the blossoms nearby. "Holy cow!" I'm knocked against a hard tree trunk.

"I'm so sorry. Those damn blossoms were making it impossible to see you."

"What?" I turn around, the tall shadow emerging from the mist of pink sets my heart into a frenzy, until I see her face. It's none other than Osamu. Why couldn't it be Mrs. Takara? Why hasn't she come yet?

125

She kneels and places her fist on her heart, "I could not resist following after you to ensure your safety. Please forgive me."

I roll my eyes, not again. "How long have you been tracking me?"

"I came to Unmei as soon as you left the castle. I couldn't risk your yokai friends sensing my presence while you were traveling, but in the village my sent is masked well enough."

I pat my palm to my forehead. "I'm fine, Miki and I are playing tag."

"I will help you find her." She forms a fist full of sapphire energy.

"Wait! I'm trying to find her, not obliterate her."

Osamu drops her hands, "This will take hours." And she's right. We trapes through the orchard well past lunchtime and there's still no sign of her.

"Perhaps she went home," Osamu suggests.

"Possibly, but there's nothing to do at home, she's the one who suggested we come out here."

Hushed sobs prick my ears. "Did you hear that?"

Osamu nods her head. "Miki," she calls out with her hands cupped around her mouth.

A woman rushes into my arms. She wipes the springy strands of hair stuck to her sweaty face, her bun hangs at the nape of her neck. "Help us, please help us."

"Slow down. What's wrong?" Osamu addresses the woman.

The woman inhales deeply, trying to steady herself. "My village is under attack by yokai."

"I'd like to help, but we are trying to find a missing girl at the moment. We can go into town and get help," I suggest.

"There's no time for that, another girl will be eaten at sunset. Your friend was probably kidnapped by the creatures. They are constantly finding more to replenish their stock. It' a miracle I escaped." She clings to the sleeves of my kimono. "I tripped over this while running here, is it your friends?" She holds up a sandal.

My heart falls to the pit of my stomach. It's hers.

"First off, what is your name?" Osamu asks.

"Izumi."

"All right Izumi, I'm Osamu and this is Rika. I'll do what I can to exterminate them," Osamu authoritatively states.

"Me too," I add without hesitation.

Osamu shoots me a glare, "No, stay here, there's no telling how bad it is there."

"I'm stronger than you give me credit, and Miki needs me." I tilt my chin upward and give my best poker face.

"As you wish." Osamu nods.

Following the woman at a brisk pace, it takes us a few hours to pass through the other side of the orchard, then several more to get to her village. As we approach the village gates, Osamu looks around in recognition. "This is Onnanoko Nomi, isn't it?"

"That's correct."

"I thought your red kimono looked familiar, all of the women who live in Onnanoko Nomi wear only red. Is it still a women-only village?"

"That's right, you know a lot about this area, are you—" The woman suddenly shoves us into a bush.

Leaves and branches scratch across my palms as I try to cushion my fall. "Ouch, what was that for?" I protest.

"Shhh. The yokai will hear you."

"What kind of demons are they?" Osamu whispers.

"Frogs." She points to the village gates where I can just make out two figures pacing. "Normally frog demons wouldn't be a problem, but that's where things get tricky in our case. They have beguiled most of the women into doing their bidding. There are a few of us who weren't affected by their spell."

"This will be a bit of a challenge. Where is the best place to start?"

"I don't know, the village is covered in yokai." She covers her face with her hands.

Osamu firmly takes ahold of Izumi's wrists and pries them away. "Rika and I have abilities beyond most humans, with your assistance we will defeat them. Where will they be keeping the sacrifice for tonight?"

Her eyes widen. "To their overseer, he's boarding in the head mistress's house. Though, we'll need to secure the pond nearby first. The frogs frequently bathe there, and they'd hear any attack we try on their leader. I will fetch rope to tie up any women who give us trouble, and clothing for you, so that you'll blend in. I'll be right back." Izumi emerges from behind the branches.

The two of us wait, watching intently as she humbly approaches the village gate. The two frog yokai standing guard greet her. She bows, and they allow her to enter.

"Why are there only women in the village?" I inquire.

Osamu whispers to me, "This village is made up of widows mostly. The women here have banded together to take care of one another. It has become a very spiritual place, the women take solace in their religion. I thought they had a protector, a fox yokai if I'm not mistaken. I wonder what happened to her?"

"I don't know, but without their protector they're an easy target. The frogs get food, shelter, and all the women they want. The best part for them is they can waltz in and take it. They're disgusting." I reply.

"You've said it." She peaks above the bushes.

"Do you see Izumi?" I ask.

"Not yet."

After a few more minutes my legs get restless. The crouching has caused my feet to tingle and my calves to cramp. Finally Osamu points to Izumi coming back. She ducks behind our thicket.

"What took you so long? I was beginning to worry they had captured you." I try not to let my irritation show through, yet the downward pull of her lips makes it evident it has.

"Sorry, I had so many creeps wanting my company." She shudders. "I had to reject them politely, it was degrading." She tosses each of us a red kimono. "These will get you into the village." We take the clothing and change into them with lightning speed. "Good, are you ready?" We all nod. "Follow me. Act natural, and whatever you do, don't look into their eyes. Just smile and keep your head down."

At the entrance a frog yokai blocks our path. They are short and fat, barely my height. Their faces are the only part of them that resembles a human.

"These are the women I told you about, the ones who wish to join our village." Izumi bows deeply to the frog demon.

"I see." The frog scans me up and down, lingering at my chest. "You may enter." A wide, crooked smile spreads across the entire width of his face with one corner pulled higher than the other.

"Thank you." Izumi bows, and we all enter. Once we are farther than ear shot away Izumi speaks, "We have passed the main guards, but we need to get over to my house to get rope. I didn't have time earlier when I came to get your clothes. Then we can go to the pond." We follow her closely. The village is swarming with frog demons. "My house is right up ahead."

"Where are you going in such a hurry?" Several frogs stumble in front of us, and Izumi bumps into the bulbous stomach of the foremost yokai.

"These are new members of my village. I'm just so excited to show them my house," Izumi tries to explain, bowing to them.

"Pretty girls like yourselves should not be without an escort. We will come with you. Then you can join us for refreshments." A frog steps beside Izumi and caresses her cheek with his webbed hand, slim trails behind leaving a shimmery goo on her face. All these frog demons are stout, slimy, green, webbed, and grotesque.

"Thank you for the most gracious offer, but we would not want to slow you down. Some of my sisters are already waiting for company at the commissary."

"If you insist," The yokai licks Izumi's cheek with a long, thin, pink tongue. Izumi forces a smile. Drool drips off his tongue as he snaps it back into his toothless mouth.

Poor Izumi, hang in there. I wink at the other frog and bow. The yokai spot women passing by, and they hastily follow.

"Come on." Izumi leads us the rest of the way to her home. Her hut is very similar to Miki and Hiroshi's in size and build but she has an actual door, not just a flap of material. The door clicks behind us, and she leans against it with her arms spread out, as if to prevent anyone else from entering. "Phew, for a minute there I thought we wouldn't make it inside."

"You're one to talk. I thought he was going to eat you," I shudder.

"Now's not the time for chit chat." Izumi opens a large cedar chest and rummages through it, retrieving a bundle of rope. "Here it is. It's not much, but we should be able to tie up at least two of them." She slides it up her sleeve.

"We can just kill them." Osamu states flatly.

"No, no, I'm not ready for that." I hardly keep from stuttering.

Izumi cuts in, "She's right. I'm worried if we kill one of them the leader will sense he's lost control of one of his minions and catch on to us."

"We'll just have to knock the other ones out then." Osamu punches her fist into her other hand.

Almost ready to leave, the door opens and another villager enters. "Are these the women who have come to help us?"

"Yes, Ren. This is Rika and Osamu. Rika and Osamu, this is Ren."

"Nice to meet you all." Ren slightly bows, and we return the gesture.

"Do you know if a little girl was brought here today?" I ask.

"I'm not sure, but I overheard some yokai saying they found their next meal in a cherry orchard. No doubt she's been brought to the leader of this band of squatters."

It has to be Miki!

"We are heading to the pond at the end of the white pebbled trail to begin the coup. Are you coming?"

"I will distract the guards near their overseer's hideout. If I can lure a portion of them away, then you can sneak in later with little trouble."

"Thank you Ren. Good luck." Izumi responds. We make our way to the pond, being stopped many times by the self-absorbed captors. What should have been a fifteen-minute walk took over an hour. The sky dims, it won't be long before twilight. "As soon as these frogs pass by, we need to duck behind that cluster of reeds and cattails, and sneak the rest of the way."

The bumbling demons pass us by, without speaking to us. I shake off my feelings of uneasiness and follow Izumi off the crunchy pale pebbled path into the midst of tall grass.

Moments later we hear splashing and loud laughter. "Stop, it's too much!" says a girl in a giggly voice.

"No one can be tickled too much," a groggy voice replies.

I reach out and tap Izumi's shoulder. "They sound happy."

"Quiet down, of course they do. The frogs have them under a spell," she whispers while clenching her fists. "It's revolting that those women are forced to be swimming around naked with those creatures." Izumi's pulls the rope taught and surveys our target. "There are three frog demons and six women. The women will fight to protect their masters. I'm not sure how we'll manage them all."

I come up with a plan on the spot. "I have an idea. There are three of us, and three frogs right?"

"Yes, what's your point?" Osamu asks.

"Why don't we offer to give them a back rub? They will come closer to the edge of the pond and we will give them a massage. Once they are nice and relaxed, we'll make our move. With only one rope we'll have to bind them up altogether."

Osamu cuts in, "Rika, activate your power and hold your fists together like this. Then slowly pull away. It will create an energy rope that you can use to tie the demons up if needed, plus it can be used as a whip when flicked."

Izumi slips the rope into her kimono. We pass a look to each other and nod that we are ready. Casually we stand, and gracefully glide to the bank of the viridescent water.

"What are you beautiful ladies doing here?" A frog swims over to the rocky edge of the pond.

"We thought that you could all use a back rub." I bend down to be eye level with the yokai. I avoid eye contact by staring between his eyes at an overly large wart.

"My shoulders are pretty tense." He says, rubbing his neck. "Hey, these women are going to give us backrubs," He calls over to the others in the pond. One starts to swim over, but the last doesn't.

"I already have someone." He tickles the girl next to him. They must be the ones I heard earlier. If he doesn't come here it will ruin the plan.

"Oh, would you really disappoint me? I'm desperate to touch the smoothness of your skin." Osamu loosens her kimono enough for her sleeve to slide off of her right shoulder.

"When you put it that way, I think I would like a change in company." The last frog demon eagerly paddles over to us. We roll up our sleeves and begin to massage their slippery backs.

"Ooh, that's the spot. You have such nimble fingers." The pressure pushes out a slimy mucous secreting from his pours. My fingers tremble and it's hard to resist the intense urge to rip my hands away.

After the frogs are loosened up, Osamu gives the sign to attack. With the nod of her head, we grab the frogs' wrists and wrap the rope around them. Osamu and I use our powers to make energy ropes, while Izumi uses the rope to tie them up. We have almost all the frogs stabilized, when the village women spring from the water.

Osamu quickly incapacitates three of the women, but the other three have already freed one of the frogs. The coward flees toward the village.

"No!" I yell chasing after the frog demon. I throw a volley of energy daggers and the frog tumbles to the ground. Making an energy whip, I thrust it forward to wrap around his ankle. I drag him back to the others, while I was gone the last of the village women had been knocked unconscious.

"Good work." Izumi ties the remaining portion of rope around him. "Now we can join Ren and take back our village before the next sacrifice is made, we must hurry." We head down a path through a bamboo forest, the trip is eerily quiet, save the crackling from our footsteps on the gravel trail.

Not a sound precedes the horde of yokai that swarm us like locusts.

"How did they know?" Izumi backs away.

"And where do you think you're going?" A green webbed hand snatches her from behind.

"You're coming with us." Another grabs my waist. The yokai drag us through the bamboo to a large building.

"Where are they taking us?" I jerk against the sticky fingers pulling me.

"They are taking us to the head mistress's house. Their leader has been living there ever since he killed Akari, the yokai who protected Onnakono-nomi."

"Shut up!" A frog lifts his hand, threatening to strike Izumi. We are shoved inside the house and thrown onto the polished wooden floor. "Here they are, just as you requested."

A giant toad sits upon a throne in the middle of the room. He is much bigger than the others and he looks exactly like a toad instead of a frog, body covered in warts with no resemblance of a human. "Excellent," his voice croaks. "We can get rid of these troublemakers once and for all. Bring the first one to me."

Izumi is yanked up to the leader. His long fingers coil around her. "But how did you know?" She struggles to get away but his grip is unwavering.

"Do you think I am stupid? But you do, don't you? I discovered that your friend Ren hadn't fully been persuaded to see things my way, so I paid her a visit. Once she was under my control, she told me all about your little scheme. How convenient for me. Now, it's your turn." He lifts his thumbs and latches onto Izumi's face; he stares straight into her eyes. Swirls of smoke spin in his eyes, a wispy cloud seeps out of his eyes and into Izumi's. She holds her eyes shut tight but it doesn't matter, soon her body goes limp. She's one of them now.

"My Lord, forgive me for my wrongdoings," Izumi apologizes. He lowers her down delicately, and she kneels onto the floor next to others bowing profusely. One is smaller than the rest, wearing a dark, blood red kimono.

She lifts her head just enough, Miki! "Miki!" I yell, but she doesn't even flinch. I call out her name again, pulling against the three frogs holding me, one on each arm, and one at my waist. I stamp on their toes, but two more smother me and pin my feet.

"Bring that one to me." He points to Osamu. The frogs haul her to his throne.

"Get your filthy hands off of me!" Osamu's hands fill with blue light. With an explosion like an ocean wave she throws the demons from her. The other yokai tremble in fear, but the toad uses his control to make them fight against her. She kills demon after demon, they push her close enough to the throne that the enormous toad latches onto her throat. She aims her beam at him, but there's no effect.

"Tsk, tsk, tsk, you thought you could get away?" He lifts her up, while her hands claw violently at his. The swirls fill his eyes and she spits on his face; the cloud soon transfers to her.

"No," I exhale. I'm the only one left. Everyone else is worshipping the yokai. What can I do? How am I supposed to defeat him when Osamu's powers were useless? They carry me over to the giant one.

"It's your turn. I saved the prettiest for last." The toad grabs ahold of me.

What should I do? I've got to come up with something! I frantically look over at all the frog waiting to see me be put under the spell of their leader. If only I can get rid of their leader, then the underlings would be a piece of cake.

"No words. Why is that? Is it because you want to live with us?" He loosens the fingers laced around me to twirl my hair.

"No!" I yell yanking free, using both hands to blast energy into his face.

"*Aaah!*" He emits a horrible screech and drops me. Clutching his face, cracks spread like veins over his entire body. With a sound like a tuning fork hitting glass, his body shatters. The shards crumble to the floor and turn to dust. The remaining yokai scramble to leave.

I annihilated him. My fingertips twitch, the urge to use my powers is uncontrollable. Without the slightest attempt on my part, the red light instinctively activates. The red flames shoot up, licking the rafters. My fingers throb with anticipation fight.

My vision is hazy, a whisper floats through the air, "Rika."

A tug on the sleeve of my kimono startles me.

"Rika!" Osamu is yelling my name.

I snap back to reality. "I'm sorry, I–" My body seethes as the adrenaline leaves along with the light.

"It's you I always knew it was you." She kneels down and places her first across her chest while bowing her head.

"Get up, please don't do that."

Her head shoots up, "But you've taken the spirit of the toad yokai. I saw it with my own eyes. Only royals can absorb the life of another. You are the princess."

My temple throbs, my breath stops. It can't be true, why does it have to be me? Why can't I be normal, on Earth or Nihon?

A tired groan startles me. I whip around to find Miki trying to stand up.

"Miki!" I rush over and put my arm under her, lifting her to her feet. My hands stop aching, and the desire for violence washes away.

"My head, it hurts so much." She cradles her head with her palms. Soon Izumi is on her feet, groaning about a headache.

"I'm glad everyone's okay," I murmur.

"How did you defeat him?" Miki asks.

I give them the gist of what happened, Osamu nods with approval. Everyone is delighted that I murdered the intruder. He was evil, but I almost wish I could take it back.

I try to brush off my guilt. "Is your head starting to feel better?" I rub Miki's temples counter-clockwise.

"A little."

"I'm sure you'll be back to normal soon." The pain must be an aftermath of the toad's spell. "Let's check on the other villagers." Outside there are many women barely able to stand, stumbling and leaning against each other for support.

Though it's getting late, they offer us dinner and celebrate. Because of the late hour we are invited to stay the night in Izumi's house, and we journey home the following day.

13

"Osamu you have to head back to the castle." I say while kicking a grey stone off toward a licorice fern.

"No, this incident is proof I must stay and watch over you."

Miki scrunches her nose, "Why do you need to guard Rika?"

"No reason at all, that's why she should return to the *palace*. We wouldn't want anyone getting suspicious about a band of females with extraordinary capabilities."

Osamu bites her tongue from arguing further and simply bows her head. We go our separate ways shortly after.

Through the orchard Miki and I travel. "That's where the yokai grabbed me." Miki points to a cherry tree with an abnormally wide trunk, a hole rotted out near the roots large enough for her to hide in.

"Miki!" A voice calls out, it sounds like Hiroshi.

"Over here!" She yells.

Hirohi bolts to his sister, a breeze following him causes the tree branches to sway and blossoms to spin like mini tornados. He hugs her tight. "I've found them," he shouts.

Okami is the first of the search party to join us. "Darn, still alive?" His steal grey eyes examine my new kimono.

"I'm so glad you two are safe." Hiroshi relaxes his shoulder, as if a weight has been lifted off. "We've been searching all night. Where have you been?"

"Onnanoko Nomi," I answer sheepishly. I regret not getting Hiroshi when this all started. He must have been worried sick.

"You girls change your mind about marriage?" He swings Miki up to prop on his shoulders

"No, I was kidnapped by frog demons who wished to offer me to the toad yokai possessing them."

He arches his neck to look at her, probably unsure whether or not to believe us. "And after you expelled the evil yokai you were given these new kimonos as presents?" He says in a joking tone.

"Yep," Miki giggles.

The search group follows us back home. Hiroshi swings Miki off his shoulders as we approach the hut, Miyu rushes out. "We've been so worried," she wraps her arms around Miki, kissing her on the head a dozen times.

"I'm fine really," Miki strains to say.

Hiroshi speaks to me just above a whisper, "Can we please talk about what really happened?"

I hope this interrogation is brief. "Sure. Miki, would you take my spare clothes inside for me?"

"Yep!" She wriggles out of Miyu's hold.

"Shall we?" He offers me his arm.

"Of course." I link onto the crook of his elbow. As my skin brushes against his, there's a zap of emotion.

"Stay out as long as you want," Miki calls from the doorway. I turn around to wave, and she flashes me a wink.

"She's such a character," I laugh.

"So where did you two *really* go?"

"Just as Miki said, kidnapped by frog demons."

His biceps flex, "You're not kidding are you?"

I shake my head.

"I had hoped it was some sort of immature prank instigated by Miki. I know she's been craving attention lately."

"Sorry to let you down."

"In a way I'm relieved that you wouldn't go along with a farce like that, but," he pauses, "I feared the worst."

His voice catches in his throat, "my life wouldn't be the same without you."

My cheeks are hot, probably turning that rosy color they always get when I'm embarrassed. "We should probably get back to Miki," I stammer.

"Relax, she's safe with Okami."

I bring my gaze to his. At times it's easy to forget that his eyes aren't normal, even his lion ears and tail fade into the background. I've become accustomed to him. A smile spreads across my lips. "I missed you too."

The conversation ends abruptly, and there is an awkward silence. He must find me so boring.

The path he has been leading me on has taken us back to the cherry orchard. Always to the orchard. Maybe it's the only place for privacy around here.

"The cherry blossoms are in full bloom." I attempt to break the ice.

"Yes, they are." He plucks a cherry blossom and places it in my hair, tucking my hair behind my ear with the flower.

He stops to admire a pink blossom, his voice becomes anxious. "Miki keeps telling me how much you like me."

"Oh." To keep myself from nervously wringing my hands, I pretend to smell a branch covered in flowers. "She's right you know." My breath clenches in my chest, I said it out loud.

He releases the flower and looks directly at me. I drop my hands down, and our eyes lock.

"I like you too, at first I wasn't sure how you felt, me being a yokai after all. I didn't want to push you away, to make you leave."

"I thought after the incident with the bear demon and the girl you saved, that my feelings were pretty clear."

"But we've barely met each other. I thought that perhaps my feelings were premature, that I was misreading you. I was worried I'd ruin things between us by acting too fast, but when you disappeared, I realized I can't waste any more time. I had to tell you."

So swept up in the moment I expose more than I'd bargained for, "I've never felt so drawn to someone in my life. There's something about you, something I can't explain."

Hiroshi takes a stride toward me and places his hand on my cheek. "A force that pulls us together."

I stare into his amber eyes, never have I noticed the swirls of brown within them. But I'm the princess, how can we be together? How do I tell him? Should I tell him?

He jerks his head upward. "Did you see that?"

"See what?" I search the sky trying to understand what he's referring to.

"I thought I saw a shadow pass over us." He shakes his head as if to clear is thoughts, and enlaces his fingers with mine. His lion ears twitch. "It sounds like a flock of birds, and they are heading this way. We've got to get back to the village."

It's just one thing after another. I nod in agreement. Hiroshi swings me onto his back and dashes back home.

Hiroshi wastes no time. "Miki get inside. Where's Miyu and Kenta?"

"They are out tending to the fields."

"What about Okami?"

"I think he went into town. What's wrong?"

"There are yokai heading this way. Go get Miyu and Kenta, and then hide in the cellar."

"But I can help," Miki stomps her foot.

"Not after what just happened in Onnakono-nomi."

"Fine," Miki huffs and hurries out to the fields.

Hiroshi readjusts my position on his back. "We need to find Okami." He runs at full speed. "The yokai— they're here!" He shouts moments before the alarm bell clangs.

When we reach the center of town, Okami is in the heat of battle. "Took you guys long enough." He punches a crow demon across the jaw.

"Hiroshi, what should I do?" I ask, overwhelmed with the innumerable amount of yokai. I'm clueless as to how I'm supposed to help without getting myself killed.

Crow demons fly above us, circling the village like vultures. They swoop down occasionally to snatch a villager, but they're only taking the women.

"Gather up all of the women you can find and conceal them." Hiroshi slides me down, before jumping onto the closest crow demon, stopping him from soaring away with a girl. These demons are similar in appearance to the one who tried to kill me when I first arrived in Nihon. What if he's here? What if this is his murder of crows?

I start to panic; keep it together Rika, you can do this. I follow after Hiroshi and grab the girl away from the crow demon. His claws rip her kimono, but she appears unhurt. I push her inside one of the huts. "Stay here. I will protect this house. I'm going to be bringing more people here, so hold tight."

"Thank you," she sobs.

I scan the hectic scene, searching for anyone who needs help. One by one, I bring people to the house to hide them from the yokai. My mind and body go into an autopilot mode, so focused on my mission that the brawling around me becomes a blur. All seems to be going according to plan, until stiff fingers dig into my arm. "It's good to see you again. How I've missed you," a cynical voice rustles in my ear.

"Who are you? Get your hands off of me!" I heave away with all my body weight, but I'm thrust around to face my attacker. It's him! He came back for me.

"Oh, you're not happy to see me? That's too bad, because you're coming with me." He spreads his towering wings and flaps hard. Clouds of dust surround us and he lifts me off the ground.

"No, stop. Put me down!" I scream as loud as I can, in response he tightens his grip on my arms. I activate my powers, but I'm unsure how to land an effective blow. With him holding me pinned like this, I can't fight back.

"Help!" I continue yelling and kicking the crow, but it has no effect. *Where is Hiroshi?* Finally, someone does come to my rescue, but not Hiroshi. To my surprise Okami is the one pouncing off the backs of crows to reach me.

Okami leaps and punches the crow demon in the head from behind. His eyes glaze over and he drops me.

We fall to the ground. Luckily, it's not too far, but the wind is still knocked out of me, leaving me on the ground gasping for air. The crow yokai struggles to stand and takes flight. He flies up high, then dives at Okami. After regaining my breath, I reactivate my powers and throw energy daggers at his back.

He screeches in pain yet continues to attack Okami. Lying there on the ground, I throw one volley after the next, not stopping. The crow knocks Okami down. He's bleeding heavily, but he twists around and stalks over to me.

Okami scrambles to his feet and blocks the crow's path to me.

"I will kill you, maybe not today or tomorrow, but I will kill you. Obviously there is more prep work for me to do. Good day, your Highness." He bows before flying away, leaving a trail of blood droplets behind. The other yokai follow his lead and depart.

Okami spins around on his heels. "Are you injured?" He hungrily examines me, like a dog drooling over a steak.

"No, just some bumps and bruises. Thank you, I need to check on the villagers." I scooch backward. I look around, Hiroshi is nowhere in sight.

Okami grabs the collar of my kimono and yanks me up to my feet. "What did he mean when he called you 'Your Highness'?"

"He's an idiot. When he first saw me, he thought I was the princess, same as you. He still thinks I am, and he won't give it up. Some people are really thickheaded."

Okami furrows his eyebrows. "Yeah, I guess so." I don't think he bought that, but he lowers me anyway when Hiroshi rushes over.

He scans me up and down "Are you okay Rika? I saw that crow carry you off. I tried to get to you, but there were too many."

"I'm fine. Okami saved me."

Hiroshi pats Okami on the shoulder. "Thanks buddy. I'm glad you were here. Hopefully you two will get along better now. We need to make a sweep of the entire village to ensure the crows are all gone."

We spread out. A few villagers require medical attention and we stop to assist. It's about an hour before we return home. When we arrive, Miyu already has food on the table.

"You always know how to keep a man happy," Hiroshi comments before devouring his rice.

"You bet she does." Kenta smiles and gives his wife a kiss.

"How bad was the attack? Were you able to kill all of them?" Miki asks eagerly, wanting all the details.

"No one died, though one villager was seriously injured, and we only killed two crow demons."

149

"Will they be back?" Miki presses Hiroshi to continue.

"I'm not sure, but my gut says they will. We need to practice for the next strike. Run drills on what to do during an attack. What do you think Rika?"

"That sounds like a great idea," I reply.

"It's settled. As soon as we're finished eating, we'll begin."

"Can I come?" Miki pleads. "I want to be a defender too."

Hiroshi pats her head. "You've been doing well in your training. I suppose you can become a defender of Unmei."

"Yes!" Miki cheers.

After lunch Hiroshi, Okami, Miki, and I all go outside to coordinate future assaults. By dinnertime, we were all so tired that we barely manage to eat dinner and crawl into bed. This new regiment continues for weeks.

14

"Has it arrived?" I awake to someone whispering. This is why people should have their own rooms; so that when everyone else wants to make breakfast, or get dressed, or talk, or whatever, I can still sleep.

"Yes," Hiroshi's voice replies. "It just came in."

"Well, go wake her." Now I recognize the other voice, it's Miki.

"But she's been working so hard, she's exhausted."

"Impossible, this date is exactly what she needs," Miyu chimes in.

"Okay, I'll fetch flowers for her first. At least she'll get a few more minutes of rest."

"Will do." Miki steps lightly along the floor, but bumps into the table shaking it. "Oops."

"He said to let her sleep," Miyu replies in a hushed tone.

Hiroshi is taking me on a date, a real date. Part of me wants to sneak outside and hide; the shy Sarah inside clings to the way things are, but the new Rika emerging pushes me to take chances in life. I reach both hands in the air and give an exaggerated yawn.

"Good morning!" Miki races to climb onto the edge of my bedroll. "How did you sleep? Are you hungry? It's a beautiful day out today. Let's get you some breakfast." Not waiting for a reply, she pulls my hand to lead me to the table. Sitting me down, she quickly serves me some fish and rice. "Here you go."

I get the urge to push her buttons a bit. I guess this is how older sisters feel, no wonder siblings don't always get along. "Thanks Miki, but I'm sick today."

"What? No, not today. I'll prepare herbs for you, I'll be right back." She grabs a wicker basket and sprints to the door.

"Wait, you don't need to go, I was only teasing."

She scrunches her button nose to give me a sour face. "That wasn't very nice."

She brushes it off easily, and waits at the table humming a happy tune while I eat. As impatient as she is, I oblige and eat quickly. Before I finish my last bite of rice, Miki has already moved on to the next step, her arms are outstretched carrying my yellow kimono with my shoes nicely placed on top.

"Here you are." Miki eagerly drops the clothes into my lap. "I'll take care of your dishes."

"Thank you." I change behind the dressing screen. "You have been such an extra help for me today, I'm curious why."

"No reason at all, I'm a nice person," is her innocent reply.

I finish dressing and comb my hair. I stare into the warped mirror. I'm so plain. Why he is even interested in me? No concealer or cover-up, I didn't use these much back on Earth, but if Brandon had asked me out on a date I would have used every beauty product known to man to make myself worthy.

Miyu, who was sweeping the floor, puts down her broom and stands beside me. She brushes through my hair with her fingers. "I know you're nervous. I'm sure you overheard what's going on, but don't worry. You're pretty and he sees that."

It's not common for me to receive compliments on my appearance, especially from a non-family member. Before I can thank Miyu for her kind words, Miki has my hand in hers. "You should get some fresh air. It's so nice out today." Miki pushes me outside, then dashes back inside the hut.

The sun is warm on my cheeks; the summer air is sweet from the smell of wildflowers. I fidget with my hair and try to focus on the scenery. Before long, Hiroshi comes strolling down the road.

He hides his hands behind his back. "Would you join me on a walk? It's such a lovely day." Bringing his hands in front, he reveals a vibrant bouquet of flowers. "I thought you might like these. I picked them in the meadow."

"They're perfect. Thank you Hiroshi." He hands me the delicate flowers, and while taking them, I brush his fingers by accident and a zing of excitement shoots up my fingertips. "Where should we go?"

"You've probably already eaten, but I have a hunch you'd prefer to eat something... a little nicer."

"Absolutely." I clasp my hand lightly around the crook of his elbow. He is so proper and such a gentleman.

"You have a lovely smile."

My heart palpitates. Calm down, it's just a compliment. "I think you have very nice," um what, abs, teeth, nose, "ears." Gosh I'm an idiot.

"What, you like my ears?" He grabs a tuft of fur at the tip of his rounded ear and tugs, harder than I would think is comfortable, but he isn't fazed by it.

Laughter escapes me. "Yes, and the rest of you as well."

"You are delightful, a breath of fresh air compared to what most people think of yokai. Even the villagers I protect, yes they want me to be there for them, but that doesn't mean they accept me. Everyone fears me to a point, except you and Miki."

Not entirely true, but I'm not going to burst his bubble. "Don't be so hard on yourself."

Hiroshi grins and performs a bow. "By your royal decree, I will never do it again."

While he chuckles, my stomach twists into a pretzel. I know he's only joking, but it's not funny to me. Especially after my enlightening trip to Onnanoko Nomi. I give a pretend laugh, and try to push away the wave of anxiety.

"I knew when I met you that it was fate." He takes a deep breath, "We will enter town shortly. There are restaurants there that we can dine at. Is there anything in particular you would like?"

"I'm not sure what's available, but anything other than rice and fish would be nice."

Hiroshi chuckles. "I have just the thing in mind." We pass people in town, and they wave ecstatically. I half expect someone to press paper or a body part into his face and ask for an autograph.

"Are they always like this?

"Not usually."

"It's like you're famous."

"Everyone appreciates what I do for them. Mostly I think they don't want me to leave anytime soon."

"I think you like the attention."

"It's a plus." He stops us in front of a modest sized building with large open windows. "Here we are."

I can almost see the aroma of the cooked food wafting out the windows. "It smells delicious."

"Miki is rubbing off on you."

"I think you're right." We both laugh.

We step up into the restaurant and sit down at a short square table. Several tables like this border the room and two very long rectangular ones crowd the middle. A young woman walks over to us.

"The usual for both of us."

"Coming right up Hiroshi," the woman replies. She must be the waitress. She bows and disappears into the kitchen.

Moments later she returns with two plates filled with ripe fruit and vegetables with chicken on the side. This is the best food I've seen since I arrived on this planet. "Thank you."

"You're welcome." He picks a pair of wooden chopsticks and hands them to me.

We chat for at least an hour while we have lunch. "Let's wander around town. There are more shops I would like to show you." He helps me up, and I wrap my arm around his before we leave the restaurant.

"Where are we off to now?"

"You will see."

"So secretive."

"It's a surprise."

We pass by a few buildings with signs out front and people hammering away on the outside shingles and roof, too damaged to stay open I guess. It doesn't take long before he guides me to the counter of another shop. Most of the businesses here have an open front to it, with simple a countertop to conduct business.

A woman stands up from her stool. "Hi Hiroshi, back again so soon! Oh, you brought a tag along with you."

Her tone drops a few notches. "This must be the lady friend you have been talking about." She leans over the counter so that her lips are mere inches from his. She quaintly smiles at me but quickly averts her attention back on her target.

She's gorgeous, tall, slender, like a super model. She has red lips, perfectly done hair and makeup; adorned in a green kimono with a red obi around her waist that accentuates her shapely body. Her eyes are deep forest green, matching her outfit.

Even her scent is charming, a rose perfume I think. She's only about a year or two older than me, but I'm childlike in comparison. With the way she's pining over him, I'm surprised she hasn't dated him in the past; at least, that I know of.

"Yes Katsumi, this is Rika. I was notified you received a shipment of those new combs you were telling me about. The ones for short hair."

"I think so, but I don't know if they will work for *her* hair. It is barely shoulder length." She complains while twirling a lock of Hiroshi's course hair.

"Please try, you don't give yourself enough credit, I bet you can make them work." He holds her hand that's been playing with his hair.

I roll my eyes, but they don't notice. If we never come back to this shop it will be fine by me. Does he do this with all the women he meets? He was kissing that girl he saved from the bear yokai right off the bat.

If he's willing to do this right in front of me, how can I be sure of what he's doing when I'm not around? Does he come here when we're not training? He must have since he ordered the combs without me. Can I trust him?

"Well, I guess so." She sighs. "Give me a minute." She reluctantly releases his hand, her fingers lingering as she drifts away to the storage room in back.

As soon as she's out of sight Hiroshi squeezes my hand and winks, though he drops it like a hot potato when Katsumi appears in the door way. She lugs a crate up to the counter and drops it on top. Rummaging through the box she pulls out several ruby red combs. "All right, come here and turn around."

Hiroshi pulls out a tall stool, similar to the one Katsumi was using, from under the counter and I take a seat. I lean back and her grippy fingers snatch my hair, she drags a comb through, yanking it harder with every stroke. "Ouch."

"Sorry. I'm trying to be careful, but it's hard to keep a hold because of your stubby haircut." Her apology is shallow. It's not the length of my hair. You're just jealous. I scooch to the back of my stool, hoping it will ease the pain of her tugging.

"Sit still or I will never get this to sit properly." If you don't stop pulling on my hair so carelessly, I'll make it so *you can't* sit properly. I try to remain still and suffer through her rudeness. "I'm a miracle worker. With all of her fidgeting I had my doubts." She spins me around to face Hiroshi.

"What do you think?" I reach my hand up to touch my hair but she slaps it away.

"You look wonderful but of course you always look stunning. Do you like it?"

"I'm not sure, I can't see it."

"Of course, you need a mirror." He looks to the girl. She gives a heavy sigh and reaches under the counter, pulling out a hand held mirror. "Thank you." He holds up the shiny, metal edged mirror. "What do you think?"

"I do like it." I strain my neck to the side, trying to see the back. The comb pulls my hair back, almost like a French twist. Katsumi's mirror is much clearer than the one hanging in Hiroshi and Miki's home.

Every flaw pops out, from the scratch on my forehead, to the dirt smudges on my nose. How can I ever live up to being the great ruler everyone expects me to be?

"We'll take it." Hiroshi thanks the girl and we depart from the shop. "Now you will have something to dress up your hair," he says proudly. "Thanks for playing along back there. She's the jealous type, and it was hard enough for her to give me a gift for another woman."

"Who is she to you anyway?"

"A friend." Hiroshi brushes off my question like it doesn't matter.

My voice heightens with agitation. "That's not how it sounded. You and her seemed pretty cozy, and it doesn't take a genius to realize she doesn't like me. Every time I turn around some girl is throwing herself at you."

"I doubt each time you change direction there is a new woman hanging around. But I'm sorry she was rude to you. I guess I'm just irresistibly handsome."

I glare at him.

He sighs. "She's had a crush on me since I came here, but I've never gone on a date with her. I have turned her down every time she's asked."

"Why?"

"Well, when I was new in town, I had more important things on my mind than dating, and then after that, it never felt right. Besides, she's too full of herself. She thinks she's so charming but honestly, she's pretty plain." If he thinks she's dull, then there's no way he can find me attractive.

Hiroshi and I spend the rest of the day exploring the village, visiting shops, and talking with the villagers.

"This has been a wonderful day. Thank you for showing me around."

"You're not off the hook yet."

"What do you mean? It's dark."

"You'll see." We follow along the dirt road toward home. Soon our home pops into view, but instead of going inside Hiroshi leads me off in the opposite direction and up a bit of a hill. At the top, he settles down on the ground. He pats the ground next to him, and I sit beside him on the cool grass.

"All right, I have to admit, this is pretty soft grass."

"What?" He laughs, a little baffled. "That's not why I brought you here." He points toward the sky. "Look up."

I lean back and gaze up into the heavens. There are thousands, maybe even millions, of stars twinkling up above. "Wow. They're amazing."

The swirls of lights, the colors of purple and red smear across the night sky, truly extraordinary. Never on Earth could I see such a sight, even if I didn't live in the city.

"Yes they are and you are right, the foliage is really nice too." We share a laugh. He places his hand over mine and asks, "Would you like to play a game?"

"What kind of game?"

"A fun one."

"Sure, tell me the rules." If this was any other guy holding my hand asking to play a fun game, I'd slap him across the face.

"Okay, so each of us takes turns finding an animal or some other object in the sky by connecting the stars, and then the other person has to try and find it."

"Sounds interesting. Why don't you go first and show me how to start."

"All right, a butterfly."

"You see a butterfly?"

"Yep."

"Okay, is it…that one?" I point to a cluster of stars.

"Nope, that's not the butterfly I see."

"What about those stars over there?"

"Not quite, but you are getting close."

I finally spot the made up constellation. "Oh, I see it! It's right there." I point to some stars just left of where I had previously guessed.

"Yep, that's the one. Your turn."

"Let's see… a cat."

"It's those stars right there, isn't it?"

"You're right. I think you're too good at this game."

He lowers himself flat on his back; he lets go of my hand and wraps his arm around me. I lie back resting my head on his shoulder. We take turns, imaging bunnies, lions, a dragon, before we both fall silent, staring at the stars.

"I want to ask you a question."

"Sure, what is it?"

"What would happen if you found out that the princess never really came back or that she was dead or something. What would you do?"

His body tenses slightly. "I'm not really sure what I would do. I suppose I would stay here with Miki and protect the village, just as I always have."

"What if you found out that the princess was good and that she wanted to use her powers to help others. What would you do?"

He chuckles, "That's unlikely, the princess is a coward. She will never come forward to help this world."

"But what if she did?"

Hiroshi turns his head to look at me. "Why all of this interest in the princess? Are you having second thoughts about helping me find her?"

"No, I want to help you. It's just that, sometimes I wonder if she will step up and take the throne. If the princess wanted to do good and was willing to fight to save this world, I would want to help her, not kill her."

"I really don't know what I'd do."

"Hiroshi–"

Someone whispers, "I think she's going to tell him that she loves him."

"Shhh. She'll hear us."

I sit straight up. "Miki? Miyu? What are you guys doing out here?"

"We were just out for a stroll, but we're going back inside now."

I can't believe the two of them. "Are they gone?"

"I think so, I heard them go inside," Hiroshi responds.

"How come you didn't hear them before?"

"I did, but by the time I realized they were walking over here, I didn't want to interrupt you. Was there anything else?"

"Oh, it's nothing." I try to brush it off.

"No, I would like to know." He presses up onto his elbows.

"It's just—" I pause for a moment. I need to think of something quick. I can't continue insinuating who I really am, there's no telling who could be listening? Nothing plausible comes to mind.

Without fully considering the outcome I blurt out, "I think I'm falling in love with you." I can't believe I just said that. Even though the night air is chilly, my face is hot and flush. My heart pounds and I try not to hyperventilate. I've screwed things up.

"You don't have to be so embarrassed. Your secret is safe with me."

I let out a sigh of relief. I'm glad he didn't say "I love you too." The only reason I blurted it out was as a cover up. I don't have a sure footing on my feelings for him. Yet, why didn't he say he feels the same way. Maybe he's just as unsure as I am; now I've probably scared him away by moving too fast. "Thanks, it's getting late though, about time we went to bed."

"Good idea." He rises to his feet and helps me up. We go home and as soon as we step inside, Miki and Miyu want to talk.

With Hiroshi's nod of approval, I spend the rest of the evening chatting with Miki and Miyu. We stay up late having girl time. I tell them about my confession of love and my embarrassment.

Of course Miki is annoyed with Hiroshi for not saying he's in love with me too. We chat through most of the night, but I don't mind since I'm too giddy to sleep anyway. We eventually fall asleep, dropping out of the conversation one by one.

15

Lately all I dream about is Hiroshi, until last night. I dreamt of home, of Mom and Dad. It's been a while since I was brought here, they must think I'm never coming back, and truth is I don't know.

I spring up in my bedroll, and of course, everyone else is already up. At least Okami didn't interrupt my sleep with one of his sarcastic comments. I comb my hair and change into my kimono.

"Good to see you're awake."

"Good morning Miyu, do you know where I can get a paper and pencil?"

"I'm sorry I don't have any. You'd have to ask Miki or Hiroshi, they went out to pick fruit earlier."

"Thanks, I will go find them." I briskly walk down the dirt road, I call out Miki's name occasionally.

It's not long before I hear a reply, "Yes? I'm over here." Off the path, Miki is balancing on Hiroshi's shoulders picking peaches.

"Hi Miki, do you have a pencil and paper?"

She reaches up and plucks a fuzzy white peach. "Sorry, paper is pretty expensive. It's been awhile since we've had any."

"Oh..." Darn it.

Hiroshi's lifts a woven basket up for Miki to plop the fruit into. "Don't worry, we can obtain them in town. What do you need it for?"

"To write a letter to my parents." Not that I have any way of sending it.

Miki glides off his back. "Are you going home?"

"No, but I want to let them know I'm doing well and that I'm safe."

Miki blows out a sigh of relief, "You two go on without me. I've got chores to do." Miki winks and dashes off.

"Shall we?" He offers me his arm. I gladly accept his chivalry, and we stroll into town. People along both sides of the street are busy repairing buildings.

Eventually we arrive at a humble shop, and Hiroshi guides me up to the counter. "Hello, do you have a pencil and a piece of paper?"

The shop keeper bows and vigorously shakes Hiroshi's hand. "Anything for you protector. It's such a relief to have you back. I worried every day you were gone, but now I know everything will be all right. Let me get you your supplies."

The shopkeeper is an older fellow, about fifty or sixty years old. Slightly hunched over, he scoots into the back room. He rustles around and returns shortly. "Here you go. I hope you'll be staying in Unmei for a while."

"That's the plan."

"Excellent, you can come back anytime for more."

"Thanks so much." Hiroshi bows, and we leave the shop arm in arm.

Hiroshi hands me the paper and pencil. "Here you are. Now you can write your letter."

"Thanks, this means a lot."

Hiroshi nods. "If there is anyone else you would like to write to, just let me know."

"I will." I smile and give his arm a light squeeze.

"Do you miss your parents? We could go visit them."

"I don't think that would be a good idea. My parents were fighting when I left, they wanted me gone. Fate took me on another path." It's the truth to a point. "There are some personal things I need to think about. I'd like to write my letter on my own, if that's okay."

"No problem. When you're ready to have your letter delivered, take it back to the shop where we got the supplies. Do you remember which one?"

"Yes." Not that I'll need to, I don't know how I'm ever going to get this back home. My only hope is to find Mrs. Takara. "Thank you so much. You've been so kind to me, too kind. How can I ever repay you?"

Hiroshi's hand gently rests on my cheek. His thumb strokes away a lock of hair. "Your smile is all the payment I'll ever need."

"I...I..." I stammer. I don't know what to say, so instead I give him the sweetest smile I can muster. I make eye contact for the briefest moment. These new emotions for Hiroshi, are causing my crush on Brandon to fade. Perhaps it's a good thing Brandon and I never dated. I would feel guilty accepting Hiroshi into my life if Brandon was waiting for me on Earth.

"I'll meet you back home when you're finished." His hand slips from my cheek; he gradually backs away, leaving me to write my letter.

As he walks away his lion tail swings back and forth. The man I am falling in love with is part human, part lion. I always imagined myself marrying the tall, dark, and handsome type, someone who would wear a tuxedo on our wedding day. Yet Hiroshi has wire golden hair, cat eyes, and wears clothes made from lion furs.

A man running brushes past Hiroshi, and stops dead in front of me, "I've been so worried about you." My heart does a summersault, it's Brandon! He gracefully whisks my hand into his, "My darling, I'm so happy you're safe." He leans close, gently he breathes, "Mrs. Takara has sent me, play along."

Hiroshi is at my side in a heartbeat, "Who do you think you are talking to her that way?" He puffs his chest, cat claws defensively extending.

He addresses Hiroshi, "My name is Jiro, and I'll be taking my fiancé back home now. Thank you so much for taking care of her." He bows briefly, then tugs me into his arms. "Let's be on our way."

"Hold on," Hiroshi's firm voice demands," Rika, is he the reason you ran away? Were your parents arguing about your betrothal? I have pondered why a girl so beautiful would not be married at your age."

"No, I, um," I stammer. What is Brandon doing here?! If he has answers I should go with him, but after what he just said to Hiroshi, I don't know if he'll ever forgive me. "Give me a minute," I hesitate trying to remember the name he gave, "Jiro." He nods and drops his arms while stepping aside, allowing me miniscule privacy.

"Hiroshi, I am so sorry about this."

"You should have told me, you led me to believe otherwise." He breathes out heavily and his nostrils flare.

"But you don't understand. I don't love him, and as far as I'm concerned he is not my fiancé. He can deliver the message to my family directly. I'll try to sort things out with Jiro. I promise to return later today."

His eyes focus on me, "Do you mean that? Will you really come back?"

"I promised you didn't I?" We share a nod before I return to Jiro. He slips his hand into mine and leads me away. I can't help but to look behind, the hurt in Hiroshi's eyes is evident, it takes all of my will power not to bolt to him.

Jiro ushers me through town and out to the cherry orchard. Once we are well inside he turns to me, "Surprise."

"What are you doing here?" His dark hair and eyes are exactly as I remember, his smile pearly-white and perfect. The only thing different is the dark blue kimono he's wearing.

"I told you, I'm your fiancé."

I laugh it off, "That was just a rouse, you really hurt his feelings you know." I attempt to scold him but I'm too excited to stay mad.

"He's yokai, it's not like they have feelings anyway."

My voice rises a few notches, "Take that back, he's different."

"He's a yokai, out to kill the princess no doubt."

I can't contest that remark. The truth in his words sobers me, but he has a good heart, I know he does. A shadow moves out from behind Jiro, it's Mrs. Takara!

She dashes to me, "How are you?"

Her voice is so comforting to me; a tear rolls down my cheek. She finally came. "I'm fine," I croak through the tears. "How are you?"

"There, there, child." She gently pats my head. She speaks in a soothing tone. "There's no need to cry." She carefully pulls me out to arm's length.

"I'm so glad you're safe, I was so worried. After the portal recharged I came as quickly as I could, but you were

170

nowhere to be found. So I went back for Jiro, and that took even more time. I just got back and immediately sent Jiro out to find you. Where have you been?"

"I found her with a yokai," Jiro answers for me.

"What?" Mrs. Takara tilts her head to the side.

"Well, Hiroshi saved me, I've been traveling with him, helping search for the princess."

"Hold on a minute. Hiroshi has recruited you to help him find the princess?"

"Yes."

Her old voice cracks into laughter. "That's hilarious. I'm sure you've come to realize who you are?"

"Yes, through a series of events."

"You're a smart one. Plus you found yourself a personal bodyguard, and a very handsome one at that."

I blush. "Oh stop, that's not the reason I've remained with him."

"Good, because I would like to introduce you to someone, you probably know him under another name, but here you are to address him as Jiro. He is your fiancé, you can't go falling in love with a demon.

"You are the princess, which means you have an obligation and duty to this world to marry from the proper bloodline. If you do not, the royal powers would cease to exist. By marrying Jiro it will ensure the strength of the royal lineage, and he will assist you in establishing and keeping peace."

My jaw drops, she's serious. "Mrs. Takara," I hesitate, unsure of what to say.

"Call me Aimi."

"How is this possible, why did you never tell me?"

"We were instructed to never reveal our identity. Our mission was to protect you and be a familiar face when you transitioned to Nihon. The main reason for keeping things hidden from you was to minimize speculation by others. Imagine if you told anyone on Earth that you're from another world, you would have been locked up. I'm sorry for the lies, but it was the best way to keep you safe and to give you a normal childhood. It's long overdue that you come live with me, where you'll be safe and I can debrief you on what will follow in the coming weeks."

"Mrs…Aimi, I need time to think. Every time I catch my footing another aspect of my life changes. I don't know how much more I can handle."

"I can give you the stability you crave. Plus, you won't be wed right this minute, it will take time to prepare, we should do the wedding just before your announcement as the princess. At that time you two will become emperor and empress over Nihon." I shake my head and try not to listen. Mom was always forcing her will onto mine, and here apparently I have no say in my future either.

I politely interrupt, "Aimi, could I write a quick letter to my parents on Earth, and can you deliver it?"

"Yes, I will set it on your old bed."

I press the paper against a mostly flat section of cherry tree trunk and scribble the note.

Dear Mom and Dad,

I miss you so much. I'm staying with a friend for the summer. Please don't be worried. I need to figure things out in my own way.

Love,

Sarah

Aimi sets her hand on my shoulder, "Are you finished?"

"Yes." The weight of her hand is heavier than it should be. It's difficult to imagine bearing the burdens that has been asked of me.

She takes the paper, her wrinkled face stiffens. "You know those people back on Earth aren't related to you."

"What?"

"They adopted you."

My chest tightens, my *adoptive* parents. "What happened to my real parents?"

"I'm sorry dear, everyone else in the royal family was killed during the rebellion."

My eyes sting. "Did I have any brothers or sisters?"

Aimi hangs her head low. "No, it was just you." She says somberly."

My body shakes, my knees lock. How could they never tell me I was adopted? Maybe they thought I wouldn't love them as much. That's Mom I guess, holding on so tightly to everyone that it inevitably pushes them away.

"All of your family was killed during the rebellion, you're the last one in your line. That's why it's imperative you leave that nonsense behind and come with me. Jiro and I will keep you out of harm's way."

I draw in a long breath. What should I do? If I stay with Aimi I would be a lot safer and I could find out more about Nihon and my past, but I would lose opportunities to serve others directly. The people I've helped is undeniable. The seer said I need to change the way people think of the princess.

If I hide away I'll be playing into the doubts many have for me. I have been out there, making a difference, proving myself. I'd have the opportunity to unite. If I sneak away to my palace, there's a good chance another rebellion will strike up, and I could be the next Marie Antoinette.

I rub the back of my neck. Back home my mom always told me where to go and what to be, but not anymore. My voice now firm, I say, "If you had asked me to join you from the beginning, I would have gone without hesitation. But things have changed."

Jiro cuts in, "You can't really want to stay with *him*?"

"It's more than that."

"Then I'll come with you."

"No." Aimi lifts up her hand. "That would complicate matters. Are you sure?"

"Yes."

Jiro takes my hand. "If that is the case, I will wait for you. When the time has come we will be wed." His words are sincere, but I can't shake how ludicrous this ordeal has become.

I return my attention to Aimi, "Before I go, can you tell me a little bit more about this world? Can I ever go home?"

"I'm glad to hear you're taking an interest in your home world. When this world was created, it was modeled off of Earth's Japan from hundreds of years ago. The lifestyle has progressed exponentially on Earth, but we choose to keep the old traditions.

"How old is this world? Who created it?"

"The planet itself is millions of years old, but life was introduced only a few hundred years ago. Legend says that every living creature was created by the first emperor and empress of this world. That is why the royal family has such great powers. With regards to Earth, I'm afraid you'll have to remain on Nihon for now. One day you'll be able to go back, once things have settled."

"I understand, I guess." Since I'm the princess I feel like I'm the one who should be giving the orders and making the rules. Aimi is only looking out for my best interests I suppose.

"My house is just south of here. If you change your mind I'll be there. If not, we'll be in touch soon. Be careful." She glances at the treetops, before giving me one last hug. She reluctantly lets me go.

"Good-bye." I wave to Jiro and Aimi. There's so much I need to learn from her; it's overwhelming. I wasn't completely honest with her, part of the reason I wish to stay is Hiroshi, and now I feel guilty about it.

Back home honesty was always my policy, but now all I seem to do is lie, I hate it. It makes me sick to think about all the friendships and relationships that are built on lies. I've been told eventually lying becomes easier, but I don't want it to become easier. I want to tell the truth.

How can I give my heart to Hiroshi if I'm constantly lying to him? Perhaps this betrothal is the wisest course.

The return trip was much shorter than I had anticipated. Miki is playing outside and cartwheels over to me. "Hi Rika, did you mail your letter?"

"Yes, Hiroshi helped me procure the supplies."

"Do you want to play with me?"

"I'd love to, but right now I need to speak with Hiroshi. Is he around?"

"No, he's assisting in the repairs of the magistrate's store house, I'm not sure when he'll be back."

"In that case, I can play until he gets back." My hungry stomach protests, but I try to ignore it. We link arms and skip around, playing tag and hopscotch. Imagination takes hold an we lose track of time, before we know it, it's nightfall.

"You guys have been gone all day. Where have you been?" Miyu inquires when we finally come inside.

"We've been playing. It was lots of fun." Miki removes her shoes and takes a seat at the table.

"I'm glad you two enjoyed yourselves. When I didn't see you for lunch Miki, I was starting to get worried. And Rika, I don't think you've eaten all day. Miki, please set the table." Miyu carries food to the table while Miki jumps up and gets the dinnerware.

"Is there something I could help you with?" I ask.

"No, that's okay." Miyu sets the pot of rice on the table.

"Just let me know if I can lend a hand." I shift my weight back and forth.

"I will." Miyu puts on a smile, but I can tell she won't ask for my help. Why does she reject my offer? Is it simply because I'm a guest, does she know more than she's letting on, or does she not trust me? With all the lying I do I wouldn't blame her. I sit down at the table while Miki fetches the men.

Hiroshi enters through the door flap and scans the room, his eyes rest on me, his shoulders relax as he lets out his held breath. Dinner is tense, I want to reassure Hiroshi I'm not going anywhere, but there's no chance with everyone else around.

After dinner while laying out my bedroll, Hiroshi comes to my side, "Rika, were you able to get your letter mailed?"

That wasn't the question I expected him to ask, "Yes, thank you so much. I'm sure my parents will be relieved to hear from me."

"I'm glad I could help." Hiroshi glances away and his voice becomes a little shaky. "Did Jiro leave?"

"Yes, there's nothing to worry about."

"Have you called it off with him?"

"It's complicated."

Hiroshi opens his mouth to say something, he shakes his head. "Never mind. I will see you tomorrow. Good night Rika."

"Good night Hiroshi." What am I supposed to do now?

16

"Today's the day! Today's the day!" Miki leaps around in the hut. "It's the Best Protector competition!"

Ugh, what time is it? It's not even light out. It's not Christmas. No one should be awake at this hour. I attempt to smother myself with my pillow. Last week we were approached by the magistrate to participate in a competition for the best protector in Unmei.

He claimed it's his way of honoring the four of us for our dedication, but I think the idea is more about boasting Unmei's defenses to encourage growth of the economy. It's a publicity stunt, but it still sounds fun. We've been practicing ever since.

"Oh Miki, control your excitement. You've gone and woken Rika," Hiroshi's voice hushes. I miss hearing his voice, most days he avoids me. I have to make things right with him.

"She sleeps too much as it is. It would be good for her to wake up early once in a while," Okami grunts.

"Oh be quiet. If you think you need to deprive Rika of her sleep so that you have a chance to win, then drop out now," Hiroshi taunts him.

"Huh, fine, let her sleep. She'll need all the help she can get," he sneers. I hear the whoosh of the door cover as he exits the hut.

"No one can sleep with this racket," I mutter through the pillow. My body protests, but I force myself out of bed and prepare for the day.

After I finish dressing and step out from behind the dressing screen, Hiroshi approaches me. "I'm sorry about the noise. You must be tired."

I hold back a yawn, our first conversation since things went south, "Don't worry. As you said, Okami is going to need all the help he can get. I'll live. An early start can't hurt."

"As always, I like your kimono, but don't you think you will need something a little easier to compete in?"

"What do you mean? I don't have much else."

"That's where you're wrong." He walks behind the table and pulls out something from underneath. "Here you go. They're gifts from the magistrate."

He reveals a set of battle armor. The armor pieces are silver and rectangular with rounded edges. They have yellow ribbons to tie to my forearms and shins. There is also a light mesh, almost chain mail, torso tunic.

I hold the outfit in front of me, "It's a bit revealing, don't you think?"

He averts his eyes and stammers, "Oh, of course. I forgot to give you the underclothing." He snatches a black combat suit from under the table. "Here, sorry about that."

"No problem." I chuckle.

He hands me the outfit and I change behind the dressing screen. I can't help but wonder what the suit is made of. It's stretchy and skintight, a lot like spandex. The armor itself takes some time for my fingers to fumble the ribbons into a knot while I hold the metal plate in place with my chin, but eventually the ensemble is complete.

"You look great." Miki beams.

"So do you." The ribbons attaching her armor are pink. She twirls around. Her outfit has a small pink skirt, which ripples each time she spins around, she's like a ballerina warrior.

Hiroshi and Okami enter the hut, both sporting their own set of armor similar to mine. Hiroshi's is green, while Okami's is blue. I've never seen them so modestly dressed. Never have they looked so human.

"Have you eaten yet?" Hiroshi inquires.

"No, not yet." It's not like I've had the time.

"We need to be leaving shortly, I'll pack you some food." Hiroshi packs pieces fish and a scoop of rice into a cloth for me.

"Thank you. I'll eat on the way." Why is he being so nice all the sudden, has he forgiven me?

I follow Miki and the others down the main dirt path. Villagers spring out of their homes and cheer for us. They trail behind us to the competition.

Girls giggle and point at Hiroshi and Okami. Boys whistle at Miki and me. All this attention, I'm starting to like it, though I have a tinge of stage freight.

I've learned new ways to control my powers, but the results aren't always spot on. I'd hate to look like a fool in front of all these people.

We come to a large field where the event is being held. Haru, the magistrate, stands atop a hill next to the field. He is a stout older man, about forty years old. He is bald but has a full black beard, speckled with gray.

"Welcome," he bows, and we all bow in return. "We are so grateful to have you all here to defend our village."

He turns to address the swarm of people that have followed us. "Welcome everyone, to our first annual Best Protector Competition. Now there are going to be three challenges for our protectors. The first challenge is the Agility Test. The second is Free-Style. The third, Sparring. Everyone, please make yourselves comfortable while I show the contestants to the starting line."

We follow the pudgy man as he waddles to the white strip of sand across the dirt track. I take a runner's pose behind the line and lift my head; before me is an elaborate obstacle course.

Yep, I definitely should have practiced more. We are the only ones competing in the contest, I have a one in four chance of winning, yet I doubt I'll come out first. Me, against two yokai and a girl blessed with acrobatics, yeah right.

The Haru explains the rules and then says, "Everyone ready?" We all nod our heads in agreement. "On your mark, get set, go!"

With that, we're off. The crowd goes wild with cheering.

Miki starts in the lead, with Hiroshi close behind. Okami is just beyond me, making me in last place. *Come on Rika.* I clear every hurdle and crawl under the net. I swing across the mud pit, and climb the cliff, but no matter what I do, I can't seem to catch up.

Okami is growing ever closer to overtaking Hiroshi, but Hiroshi holds his lead. Miki passes behind the white post first, then Hiroshi. I expect Okami to be the next one behind the post, but he slips by in front unnoticed. He cheated! He didn't go behind the post. The judges are too focused on Miki and Hiroshi to notice.

I have more integrity than that schmuck, so I race behind the marker in a futile attempt to catch up. At this point, everyone else has already started their descent down the cliff, and they are no longer in view.

I definitely needed more training. I continue through the obstacle course and push myself hard until the end. I cross the finish line with everyone waiting for me.

I rest my hands on my knees and try to catch my breath as my chest heaves in and out. Miki bounces around ecstatically and performs a flip tuck, she must have placed first. I congratulate Miki and bite my tongue about Okami's cheating, he'd just deny it.

"And Rika comes in fourth place in this event," Haru announces. He gives us the rules for the next event. "Understood? Okami, you're first, the rest of you will take seats next to the audience."

Okami enters the ring for his freestyle performance. He is calm and collected, his face relaxed. I've never seen him like this before, so zen.

Focused on the task ahead, he begins his routine. He accomplishes a variety of complex attacks and moves that wow the crowd. I'd hate to get in a fight with him. He concludes his routine with a high jump-kick attack. The crowd goes wild shouting his name.

"Next up, Hiroshi," Haru announces.

"Good luck," I whisper to him before he takes his place on the field. His routine is similar to Okami's in complexity, but with flare and more interesting moves. The audience loves him. I think Hiroshi has him beat on this one.

As Hiroshi ends, many of the villagers leap to their feet applauding his performance. Okami just sits there, pretending not to notice. What a lump, he can't be happy for his friend. I hope he loses.

Hiroshi takes a seat next to me. "How did I do?"

"You were amazing!" I smile and give him a hug. The tension between us has vanished.

"Next up, Miki."

She jumps up. "Wish me luck." She skips over to the field and begins her routine with a cartwheel. Miki has many thrilling moves, much different than Okami or Hiroshi.

She plays up her acrobatics powers to the max with handstands, somersaults, cartwheels, front flips, back flips, and many more very complicated tricks combined with attack moves.

"Truly amazing, isn't she?" I exclaim.

"Yes, she is," Hiroshi says as he applauds loudly. The crowd claps and cheers her on with each agile move she performs. She performs her finale, and the villagers burst into applause.

"You were great Miki!"

"Thanks Hiroshi. Looks like it's your turn now Rika. Good luck." She takes my place as I rise.

"Last but not least, Rika."

"You can do it," Hiroshi encourages. I nod and step onto the performance arena. I start mine off with some simple moves, like making the red light appear in my hand for punches.

I gradually move on to more complex moves where I use my energy as a whip. Then I add energy daggers, and increase my speed. I add in a few new tricks I've learned, and for my last move, I throw as many energy daggers into the air as I can directly above me and then create an energy shield bubble.

The energy daggers rain down on my energy shield, exploding with a rainbow of colors as each one hits. The daggers shatter into tiny pieces and softly float to the ground like confetti. They disappear into a fine dust and vanish.

Totally focused on my routine, I hadn't realized the hysteria from the audience. They are jumping and cheering,

185

Haru is holding his hands up to keep them from swarming the field. I hope this makes up for how poorly I did on the obstacle course. As I step off the performance arena Miki runs up to me.

"That was so cool! I think you've won this one."

"All right, settle down. I need a moment to consult with the judges and determine the placement of the contestants," Haru announces as he approaches the judges' table.

"You'll get first place for sure," Hiroshi assures me.

"I don't know. Miki's routine was very impressive. I think she will take first," I reply, trying not to get my hopes up.

"Quiet down. I have the placement results. In fourth place, Okami." The crowd claps for him, but he rolls his eyes and crosses his arms. "In third place, Hiroshi." The audience cheers, and I give Hiroshi a quick hug. "In second place, Miki." The crowd stands and applauds.

Miki grins and shakes my arm. "This means you've won first on this one!"

"In first place, Rika."

The spectators chant my name. I've won. I've really won. I can't believe I actually won something.

"Now, on to our last round, Sparring. Contestants, please come up to the performance area for the rules." He explains we need to hit our opponent in the torso five times to win. "Be careful. Does everyone understand?" Haru stares at us, his eyes very serious. We all nod in agreement. "The first match will be Miki against Okami."

They take their place on the field while Hiroshi and I sit down next to the villagers. "I guess this means we will be fighting against each other next." I look over at Hiroshi. "Don't think I will go easy on you," I kid. We both give an awkward chuckle and then turn our attention to the pending battle.

"Ready, set, go!" Haru yells. Miki is graceful, dodging Okami's every attack. She glides behind Okami and punches. "That's one for Miki." She evades him expertly. She executes a perfect somersault and punches his side rapidly three times. "Three more for Miki! One more hit and Miki will win." Miki grins and prepares herself for her next move.

"Go Miki!" I shout, leaping to my feet. She springs behind Okami and winds back her arm for the final hit when he dodges and slams his fist into her chest. Oh no! She falls to the hard packed dirt with a sickening thud. Okami raises his hand for another blow, his eyes filled with rage.

"No Okami!" I yell, running to protect Miki. I throw energy darts at his wrist, preventing him from pulverizing her, he recoils his hand in pain.

"Can't you see she's injured? Why would you use that much force on a little girl?" He backs away. Miki is curled up on the ground with her arms in the shape of an X. Hiroshi is immediately at her side.

"Time out!" Haru shouts as he rushes to us. "Okami, that was overkill. Is she all right?" He asks.

Hiroshi presses against her chest, and she winces. "I think so, but she cannot finish the match." He says.

"Both of you forfeit the match. Okami because you used too much force and Miki because you are unable to continue. That means that it's between Hiroshi and Rika. But first, Miki needs to be escorted to a safe place." Haru waves for someone to help.

A woman sprints over, Hiroshi scoops Miki into his arms. "This is my wife. She will take care of Miki while you two battle." She follows Hiroshi off the field.

"Thank you Haru." I bow out of admiration. Some earn status through respect, instead of fear.

"As for you, Okami, take your place in the crowd." Haru swats Okami away with his hand. He stomps off the field. Hiroshi returns, it's our turn to spar. "Now, let's have a clean match this time. Ready, set, go!"

Hiroshi charges toward me, I freeze for a moment and a thought flashes through my mind, is this how it will be if he ever finds out? His intentions are good, but he's still yokai. I shake my head and position out of the way barely in time, while taking the opportunity to hit him twice on the back lightly with my fists.

"That's two for Rika."

He turns and advances again. I attempt to dodge, but he moves with me and hits me three times in the stomach. I'm glad he's not hitting very hard or I wouldn't have been able to make it through that volley. It's time I go on the offense.

I race toward him and create an energy shield, ramming him with it. He's knocked back, dazed for a few moments, and I use that time to get him twice in the back. I try for a third, but he hits me inches below my armpit.

This is it. I stand my ground as I watch him barrel toward me for the final time. I put up my energy shield to block him, though he doesn't fall for that one again. He dashes to the side and reaches for the last punch, I block him with my forearm just in time.

While still close, I attempt to hit him in the chest, but he stops my hand. We exchange blocking and hitting in close combat for several moments until he slides his leg behind me and trips me. I clumsily grab onto his armor, and he falls on top of me. He swiftly scores the last hit to my side, but he's very gentle about it.

"Hiroshi is the winner of this event!" Haru yells, but Hiroshi and I are too focused on each other to care.

He smiles and leans in closer, I flutter my eyes shut. I can almost feel his lips on mine. *Just kiss me already.* The noise of the villagers grows louder, they must be coming to congratulate us.

Come on Hiroshi, we don't have all day. My heart thumps in my chest, drowning out the background noise. I feel him push himself off and I open my eyes. I lay there on the ground only momentarily before he takes my hands and pulls me to my feet.

"Now, all of the contestants please come to the field so I can announce the winner." We all line up in a row next to Haru on the field. Miki manages her way to the field, limping slightly. "In third place, Okami. Tied for second, Rika and Miki. In first place, and the winner of our Best Protector Competition, Hiroshi!" Everyone, except Okami, explodes with excitement and Haru congratulates us.

"You were great! You deserved to win." I hug Hiroshi, who is in shock about his victory.

"We were all great." Hiroshi lifts me into the air. Everyone is pumped with energy and excitement, except for Okami. "Let's return home and celebrate."

"Sounds like a plan to me." Miki smiles past her pain.

I offer her my arm for support but she declines. "How are you feeling?"

"I'm fine. I will be back to normal in no time," she says through a wince.

I glance from Miki to Okami. His face is solidified with a grimace. I bite my tongue and head over to the path home.

After only a few steps, several villagers stop us to congratulate Hiroshi on his accomplishment. While Hiroshi converses with his admirers, Jiro approaches me. "Could I speak with you for a moment?"

"Excuse me," I stutter. "I will be right back," I tell my companions, but only Miki acknowledges that she's heard me. Has he been watching this whole time? I follow him a ways off, until we are alone in the shadows of three large pine trees.

"That was a magnificent show, you really should have won." He places his hand on my shoulder, "It's time to come home Rika, time for us to be wed and for you to announce you title."

A lump forms in my throat, "But I thought there wasn't any rush. I've hardly had time—"

"Time for what? Stop making excuses, you displayed your skills well today, you should be proud." Jiro leans in, attempting to kiss me on the lips.

190

I shove him away, "What are you doing?"

"You are my fiancé, I'm just trying to get used to this new step together."

The burden of being royalty has never hit harder. My duty is to marry Jiro, an obligation I don't want to acknowledge. Risking my life to help others is an honor, but I am apprehensive at the thought of sacrificing my heart for this world.

Unfazed by my rejection he brushes my hair behind my ear fondly. "Aimi sent me to check on you. After that display you just gave, we need to speed up the timeline. I understand you want time to mentally prepare. Use this chance to say good-bye to your friends, to tie up any lose ends, we won't be seeing them for a while. I will return in a few days to fetch you."

He kisses me again, passionately. This time I don't push him, my lips relax in an attempt to test if I can ever accept my fate to be his bride.

He pulls away and bows, "Until we meet again." He spins on the heels of his sandals and strolls away. A tear runs down my cheek, if I had to, if the world depends on it, then I will marry him; until that time comes, I will force him out of my mind.

Rejoining with the others, Hiroshi notices my tear stained cheek, "What did he want?" he asks suspiciously.

"It's nothing," I turn away, but he grabs my arm.

"You wouldn't cry over nothing." His grip is frim, but his voice is gentle and low, barely above a whisper.

"He wants me to return with him, to honor my obligations, but I can't I just can't."

Hiroshi pulls me into his arms, a lock of hair sticks to my wet face, "Do you love him?"

"No."

He squeezes me tight. "While I'm around you never have to do anything you don't want to."

If only that were true, I force a smile trying to take comfort in his words, though it doesn't last long. He can't promise that, no one can. We all have to do things we don't want to sometime or another in our lives, it's just a fact of life…

17

Today is not my day. I slept terribly, my dreams filled with the impending arrival of Jiro. It's been several days since the competition and he's due back any time now. On top of that, Okami has been pressing Hiroshi to leave with him to search for the princess.

If Okami gets his way they won't be back for a long time, even worse is Hiroshi is considering it. If Jiro comes while Hiroshi is away, I'd have to go with him and I would never get to say good-bye.

I chose to take a walk in the woods to clear my head, I thought getting fresh air would help me relax. The sky was still sapphire blue when I left the hut this morning, all was going well until I became entangled by long wispy strands of a spider's web.

I yanked away but all that preceded to do was dump a large pile of spider silk on top of me. I shoved the web off and a prick of pain pinched my chest, something bit me!

I felt the arachnid wiggle up and out of my kimono, but I never caught a glimpse of it. After freeing myself, I was fine at first, but soon dizziness set in, and that's when I knew that today just wasn't my day.

I bump along the trees and try to make my way out of the forest. My feet heavily drag on the pine needle laden ground, I need to find help, and quickly. I don't think I'll make it home; I'm tripping over pine cones, at least I think they're pinecones.

What's happening to me? I clutch the bark of a nearby tree. I can't move my legs! My knees buckle and I collapse. "Hiroshi, I need your help. Please help me." I summon all my strength to call for help, but my voice is only a mere rustling in my throat. My vision blurs, and everything goes dark.

My arms are lifted and suddenly I'm off the ground. "Rika, I'm taking you home." I'm saved; someone is rescuing me.

"I can't feel my legs," I mumble.

"Don't worry, you're safe now." The voice sounds male, but I can't pinpoint who it is. The sound of his footsteps grows more distant every second, yet his pace has increased considerably. My head bobs up and down against his arm. I try to open my eyes, instead I lose consciousness again.

When I awake, I see wooden beams spinning above me, I blink hard and the room stops churning. "Where am I?" My numb lips hardly form the words, my voice is muffled. I want to sit up but I can't move my arms. "What's happening to me?"

Miyu is at my side, wiping my forehead with a cool cloth. "Calm down, I can't understand what you're saying. Jiro found you in the forest. It seems you are paralyzed. Try to relax, Hiroshi will leave shortly to get the doctor from Igaku. Everything will be all right."

Jiro rescued me? I've been dreading his return, but if it weren't for him I would be lying on the moist mossy ground of the forest dying.

"Is she awake?" Hiroshi is now at my side. "How are you doing?"

"She can't answer you." Miyu pats the cloth on my neck.

"Maybe you can't understand her, but I have better hearing. Rika," he picks up my hand, "I know this must be scary for you. I will be leaving to get the doctor from Igaku. He will cure whatever is wrong with you."

"I was bit by a spider, I think." The words come out muttered.

"You were what? I almost heard it. One more time," he squeezes my hand and encourages me to try again.

I use every ounce of willpower to make my lips move. "Spider."

"You were bit by a spider?"

"Yes."

"Good job. The doctor will use this information to ensure he brings the right medicine with him. Miyu, help me find the wound."

"Of course." Although I can't see what's happening, I feel tugging on my clothes. "How did you get a spider down your kimono?" I try to answer but Miyu places a finger to my mouth, "Shhh don't worry about explaining that now, you can tell us later."

"That is a large welt," Hiroshi exclaims.

"It doesn't look good." She pushes lightly around the bite, several inches below my collarbone. "Her skin is swelling. We need to stop it right away. Miki, fetch me more cold water and towels."

"I'll be right back." Miki is always so helpful. Would I have had a little sister like her if my Nihon parents and I had stayed together, if they weren't murdered? My thoughts wander into a dream about my parents. Their outlines form, and details fill in. Dad is in a blue kimono, and mom in a red. Before their faces are clear, I'm interrupted.

Hiroshi's voice brings me back to the present. "I'll be back soon. It should only take me a few hours to get the doctor and bring him back. I'm sorry we don't have a doctor in our village anymore. I'll return as fast as I can. Good-bye Rika." Hiroshi kisses my hand and leaves.

"Don't worry, we'll take good care of you." Miyu pats my hand.

"Here are the supplies." Miki is now at my bedside.

"Good, we need to carefully place them around the wound."

An icy cold burning sensation racks through my chest. "Ouch, it burns!" The cold cloths hurt more than they help. If I must die, let me die in peace.

196

"I can't understand what you said." Miki leans over me. "I will get Okami. Since he's yokai he should have better hearing, just like Hiroshi."

"Where is he?"

"Outside somewhere. He's always wandering off by himself."

"Go find him as quick as you can, and come right back."

Miki nods and disappears from my sight.

"I'm so sorry that we can't hear what you're saying. Okami will be here soon though." I'm paralyzed, not deaf. I can hear everything you guys are saying. My head is fuzzy and my vision is blurry, but my ears work just fine. My frustration dissipates and I feel groggy, a nap will pass the time while I wait.

"Rika, wake up! Hang in there," Someone speaks to me, everything is floaty and garbled, like I'm under water. My vision focuses enough to notice that Miyu is shaking me.

"What?" I groan.

"You're awake, thank goodness," she sighs in relief. "I was so worried that you were going to slip into a coma."

"We're here," Miki announces, entering the hut. That must be Miki and Okami. My skin doesn't burn anymore, so there's nothing to tell him.

"What do you want?" He demands, standing next to my bed. He looks much taller from this angle.

"Nothing."

197

"You're pathetic. I don't have time for this." He turns to leave.

"Stop," Miyu pleads, "we can't hear what she's saying."

"She doesn't want my help."

"I bet you can't understand what she's saying. I always thought Hiroshi was better than you," Miki taunts.

"What? You think he's better because he can hear the mumbling of a deranged girl? I can hear her, even all the way up here."

"If you really can, then prove it by staying and communicating for us," Miki challenges.

"You are such a brat. Fine, I will stay and babysit." He flops down, legs crisscrossed on the floor at my bedside. "Is there anything you need?"

I focus intensely to speak clearly, "Sleep."

"Well, take a nap then," Okami replies.

"Last time, Miyu gave me whiplash."

"Quit shaking her. She's going to take a nap."

I close my eyes and let the venom drift me off to sleep.

"Rika, can you hear me?" I lift my heavy eyelids. My head throbs, and I can barely make out the outline of Hiroshi kneeling next to me. "I've brought the doctor from Igaku. He's here to heal you." Everything pulses and aches. No matter how hard I try, I can't respond.

"Now let's take a look," an older man's voice calmly states; then someone removes the cloths on my spider bite. "Oh dear, this is a bad one." The man, who I assume must be the doctor, pushes and prods; the pain surges through my chest like needles.

The doctor examines me for another minute or so before stating, "This is one of the worst spider bites I've seen. I'll have to cut it open and extract as much venom as possible. Then the medicine will be applied, I have herbs you'll need to put on the wound periodically afterward. I'm not sure if this will save her life, but it's the best I can do." The doctor leaves my side but is back all too soon. "I'm sorry, but this is going to hurt."

I tense up, but nothing can prepare me for the pain.

"Ah!" I scream from deep within my throat as the knife slices my skin. The excruciating pain builds more and more as the doctor pushes on the incision.

Never have I wanted to die to end my suffering before. The agony becomes so intense I want to vomit, thankfully instead I pass out. Later, I awake to the doctor cleaning my wound.

"Well, at least she didn't have to feel all of that. I have done what I can. Make sure these dressings are changed every three hours and apply fresh herbs each time. All we can do now is pray that she will get better. May the ancestors watch over you." The doctor stands up and leaves my side.

Hiroshi takes his place. "I'm going to take the doctor back to Igaku, I promise to return quickly."

My head, it hurts so much. I think the doctor made things worse, not better. Am I going to die? I wish my

199

parents were here, they could take me to a hospital with all the latest medicine. What if I die from something easily curable on Earth? I try to inhale deeply, but my chest is freezing up. Instead, I take shallow breaths to survive. If I can't breathe, it'll be over.

"Just relax. I'm giving you water. Try to swallow." Miyu lifts my head and places a cup to my lips. She opens my mouth and slowly tips back the cup. I barely manage to choke it down. "Good job. Now get some rest. You'll be all better soon." I take her advice and fall back asleep.

I have no sense of time or how long I've slept for. Wild dreams have been racing through my mind, but I can't remember any of them. I regain consciousness to the sound of people talking.

"How is she?"

"Not good. Her breathing is becoming slower and more labored. I'm not sure how much longer she'll be able to hold out." That sounds like Hiroshi and Miyu. Why did she say I'm not doing well? Why can't I breathe? What's happening? Something transpired, but I can't remember.

"She's awake." He races to me. Leaning over, he brushes a lock of hair away from my sweaty face. "How are you?"

"What happened?" I barely move my lips. Why can't I talk?

"Remember, you were bit by a spider. I brought the doctor here earlier and he patched you up. You're going to be just fine." He holds my hand.

It all floods back to me, like a fan has blown away all the clouds covering my memory. I'm not fine though. Why do they bother lying?

"Rika, can you still hear me?" He rubs my hand with his thumb.

I attempt to answer him, though the words won't come out. My mouth refuses to move. I can't muster a single noise. This is it. This is the end. I'm glad Hiroshi is here with me. I would hate to die alone. With all this pain, death is almost welcomed. I relax all my muscles and prepare for the end.

"Rika, Rika?" Hiroshi squeezes my hand tight, his voice becoming panicked. "You can't die. I need you. I need you to stay here with me. I don't know if you can hear me, but I need you to keep fighting for your life. Don't give up. You must stay with me, because …because I love you. I've never loved someone like I love you. Please don't leave me."

He rests his head on my shoulder. "I will stay here with you if you will stay here with me."

A pang of emotion courses through me, *I love you too*. This is what it feels like to be in love, to care for someone so much it hurts to be apart. He's promised to stand by my side, no matter what, I have to hang on, if only for him.

He lies down next to me, continually holding my hand through the night.

The sun streaming on my face through the windows rouses me. To my surprise, my head is no longer throbbing. Hiroshi is still at my side, fast asleep. His expression is soft and peaceful, his blonde eyelashes sparkle in the morning sun.

Miyu notices I'm awake. "How are you feeling?"

"Much better," I groan.

"Wow, you must be, I can finally understand you. Is there anything I can get you?"

"I'm hungry, thirsty, and I really need to use the restroom."

Miyu laughs. "I'm sure you do." She gets me a make shift bedpan cut from a wooden bucket. Afterwards she goes to the shelf and retrieves several pillows. "These will help prop you up. I will be right back with the food."

I wiggle around in my bedroll trying to get comfortable. Someone yawns. Startled, I peek over.

Hiroshi blinks open his eyes. "What time is it?" After his proclamation last night I'm a bit nervous what his reaction today will be. He glances around the room and looks to me, "You're all right!" He grins and squeezes my hand. "I knew you'd pull through. How are you?"

"Better, but I'm so sore, and exhausted."

"Even after all that sleep? Don't worry, it will get better. I'm going to change your dressings for you. It will only take a minute." Hiroshi reaches next to him, picking up the supplies the doctor left. Carefully he begins removing the soiled bandages.

Being more aware of things now, I realize how awkward it is that my kimono is open, and there's not much fabric keeping me modest, not to mention he's the one seeing my wound in all its gruesome glory. I'm a bit mortified but I'm thankful the spider didn't bite me a few inches lower.

"Do you remember much of last night?" He inquires before pulling off the last bandage.

"Not really, it's all fuzzy," I lie. *I'm just not ready to deal with my feelings for him yet.*

He pauses his work briefly. "Oh." His tone drops. "I'm glad you are feeling better now." He continues quickly. "There, all clean. Are you hungry? Is there something I can get for you?"

Miyu bends over me. "I've got it covered." She holds a bowl of broth in her hands. "If you'd like, you can feed her the broth." She passes him the bowl.

"Where is Jiro? I want to thank him for helping me."

"Miyu sent him home right after he brought you here. He wanted to stay, but it would have been too crowded."

"Oh." He spoon feeds me a sip of broth. He stayed by my side, just as he promised, and I'm going to do the same, no matter what it takes. "Hiroshi, could you tell me a story?"

"It's the least I can do." He tells me stories about this world and the royal family while I slurp the soup, until I drift off to sleep.

18

"I wish we could come with you." Miki tugs at Hiroshi's fur loin cloth, she digs her heals into the soil and he drags her along. Two ruts trail behind her and the furs keeping Hiroshi covered pull taut.

He crouches down to eye level with her. "You need to stay and take care of Rika while Okami and I are away. This is a good lead for us in finally finding the princess and we won't be gone long. Besides, what if the she comes here while we're gone? Keep an eye out for me."

"I guess you're right." She sniffles. *If I wasn't still weak from that spider bite, we would be going with them.*

"Good-bye, we'll miss you." We wave good-bye as they depart down the road. Hiroshi promised he'd stay with me if I stayed with him. It's been over a week since I was bitten by the spider. I doubt he's forgotten what he said. Maybe it only applies if *I* remember.

"A rumor about the princess being in the forest of Shinrin, who comes up with this stuff?" Miki complains.

"If that man hadn't come here today spreading lies about a princess sighting, they never would have gone. They'll be back soon. There's no sense worrying over it." I slowly stand up, still weak from my spider bite. I haven't had a proper bath since I was bitten. I feel so gross. "I'm going down to the river to take a bath."

"Do you want me to come with you?" Miki stands ready to catch me in case I fall.

"No, I'm fine. Besides I need time alone."

Miyu interrupts, "You haven't regained all of your strength. I need to do laundry today, so Miki and I will meet you down there in a little bit. I don't want to leave you alone for very long."

"Ok." I stretch my arms up and smell the stench of my under arms, phew! "My clothes need washing as well."

"Here take this." Miyu passes me a handful of dried nuts. "They'll help." Um, ok. Help with what? The body odor?

"Thanks. See you guys later." I cautiously choose the placement of my feet as I descend the small dirt hillside to the river. My balance isn't the greatest since the incident with the spider, but I manage to arrive at the river unhurt.

I look around to make sure no one else is here before undressing and slipping into the water. I'm glad it's warm out because the water is freezing. I only dare to wade in as far as my calves before washing. There's so much grease built up in my hair, this is going to take a while.

I eventually discover that the nuts Miyu gave me create suds when I put them in the water. This makes washing my hair and clothes much easier. After getting all clean I sit on the shore and relax while my kimono dries.

My blue polka dot underwear is becoming faded and worn. You'd think the princess would get new undergarments once in a while. While staring at my poor underwear I become very tired, washing my clothes was exhausting. Without realizing it, I fall asleep on the bed of pebbles.

Suddenly, I'm awoken by furry arms grabbing me. "What's going on?" I mumble half awake.

"You're coming with me."

"No I'm not!" I try to activate my powers, but nothing happens. What do I do? I try again frantically without success. The spider bite's venom must have affected me in ways I hadn't realized.

"Shut up or I will make your day worse," a gruff voice snarls at me. I'm being carried over his shoulder. The only thing I can see from this view is his hairy feet.

"Where are you taking me?" I demand. I'm slapped in the face by a tail. Why has this yokai kidnapped me? Was it simply to kill a human or does he *know*?

"Our journey will end here if you don't be quiet!" His tail slaps me again.

I'll show you who needs to be quiet. I'll get my powers back and use them to tie up that tail—

"I can hear what you're thinking and yes I know you're the princess, and no if you try to use your powers against me, I will kill you on the spot."

If this yokai is able to read minds, I'd better be careful what I think about.

"Can't you fall asleep or meditate, unless there is any valuable information you would like to share?"

How am I supposed to sleep at a time like this? I wouldn't share any information with you, even if I had any.

"Figures, good thing I'll be getting rid of you, soon enough."

"And what do you mean by that?"

"If it will shut you up, I will tell you. I am going to use you to lure demons out of hiding. I will eat the life right out of them. Once I have done that, I will kill you. Then I will take my place as ruler of this world."

"Why would you do something like this?"

"Why? It's not like you'd care!" his voice booms. "I worked as a protector for the palace. My entire family did. For generations, my family protected the palace and the royal family, and for what?

"When the rebellion rose up, my entire family gave their lives trying to save the emperor and empress. I deserve to live in the royal palace. I deserve more than scrounging around the forest for scraps. It's the royal family's turn to repay me and my family for our service, and you're the one to do it."

"If you help me, you can live in the castle, and you can be a royal protector." There's hesitation in his stride.

"I'm done serving others. It's time for others to serve me." He shoves me further up his shoulder and quickens his pace to a sprint.

"How did you recognize me?"

"You told me princess, when you were at the river. Your thoughts were loud and clear. Now shut up."

Where is he taking me? He ignores my thoughts and presses on. The forest trees gradually change from the average pine trees, to towering deciduous; their trunks as wide as a car.

About ten minutes later, he climbs up a tree and tosses me onto a platform made out of branches. Splinters scrape into my bare thigh. I hug my knees and cover myself with my arms.

For the first time I have a view of his face. He's a monkey yokai. His human face, with an extraordinarily wide nose, is surrounded by fur that continues down his neck and onto his arms.

"Stay here and stay quiet. I'll tie you up if I have to." He stands between me and the trunk of the tree. "Here," He tosses me my kimono and sandals, "cover yourself. I'll be back momentarily. I can hear your thoughts from a distance, if you even think of escaping I'll kill you.

That's one heck of a dilemma. If I try to get away and he kills me, I stay and comply and yet again the outcome is death. I'll have to figure out a third option.

He climbs down the tree with ease. I peer over the edge of the platform, we're high off the ground. I've always been afraid of heights. I grab my garments and scooch to the center of the quaint deck, it's only about five feet by five feet. The boards squeak under the stress of my weight, very reassuring.

I dress and lay back. Gazing up into the canopy of the tree, I'm in awe of the size of the branches and leaves. It's enormous, something I would expect to see in a rainforest. I fold my arms across my chest, I've been captured. Great, but I can't think of escape, or it will seal my fate.

I try to push off thoughts of getting away, and soon enough the monkey is back.

"They will come, any time now. I've hired a messenger to send word about your capture. For real this time."

I guess all there is to do is wait, for what I'm not certain but whatever's going on isn't good. I pass the time by examining the green star shaped leaves that float down to me on occasion. I follow the veins of chlorophyll like a maze, sometimes I pretend they are a map, when I'm really bored I count them.

What felt like hours was probably a mere thirty minutes, when rustling comes from below. "Ah, my first victim." The monkey crouches low on the wooden planks, flicking the tip of his spun out tail.

I hear a pack of hyena yokai cackling and bragging about what they will do once they find the princess. It sends a shiver down my neck.

The monkey pounces down and tackles them by surprise. Horrible screeches fill the air, and the scent of blood wafts up to me. Who won? I try to see down, but they're directly under me. My question is answered moments later when the monkey demon returns grinning and breathing heavily.

"Ha, they were nothing. With each one I destroy it makes it that much easier to conquer the next." He rests against the tree trunk and slides down to a branch, his eyes crimson.

We wait in silence the rest of the day, but no one arrives. How long will I be kept as bait?

"Don't worry, you won't have to wait long." The demon tosses me a piece of dried meat. "Here, make yourself comfortable." He lights a stubby yellow wax candle.

"Thanks, I think," I mumble, picking up the jerky. Chewing slowly I peer at him over my food while he concentrates on picking fleas out of his tail. His family used to protect the royal family and now he's plucking bugs from his fur? This poor man, I wish there was something I could do to help him, to make him change his mind.

"What are you staring at?" The monkey drops his tail to glare at me.

"Nothing." I quickly pretend to examine the back of my hand. "I was just wondering what your name is."

"That's not what you were thinking."

"Well, I would like to know."

"It's Saru," he replies, picking at his tail again.

"Saru, thank you for the food. It's nice to finally have a name to call you." I force a smile.

"You're welcome. I'm sorry I don't have more to give you."

"It's fine. I wasn't that hungry anyway. So, how long will we be here for?" I speak in the friendliest tone I can muster.

"A few days at best. I would off you now, but the scent of your blood would only scare them away. Plus yokai will run for the hills once I've absorbed your powers. Right now they are conveniently coming to me. I want to make the most of this." Saru's expression is less enthusiastic than before.

"Oh, okay. At least I'll have a few days to convince you not to kill me." I nervously chuckle. I yawn and stretch my arms. "Good night." I curl up for warmth and attempt to use my hands as a pillow.

"Good night Princess." He blows out the candle.

The night goes on forever. I toss and turn on the cold hard floor of the platform. I should try to escape. He's snoring so loud I doubt he'd hear me.

I carefully prop myself onto my elbows watching Saru intently. I hold my breath, but a pair of startling green eyes flash open. He's ready for my attempt. I shiver and roll over, trying to forget about my freedom.

That was the worst night's sleep I've ever had. I'm not sure how many times I've thought that, but this must be the worst. I can't wait to get home and get descent rest. I reluctantly sit up and try to stretch out the kinks in my back. The sky is still dark and Saru is nowhere to be seen. Is he gone?

"I'm down here." He's on the ground, next to a campfire cooking.

"Good morning. Whatever you are making smells great!" I force myself to state enthusiastically.

"I found eggs nearby. It's this or nothing."

"That sounds wonderful. I love eggs." Now is a good chance to test if I can climb down this tree. I grab ahold of a vine that twists around the tree. I use the net of vines to descend the trunk and take deep breaths to prevent myself from hyperventilating. I lose my footing and my sandal slips falling the last couple feet.

I land on my bum with my heart pounding, graceful as always. I dust myself off and look around, there is blood splatter everywhere. Where did he put the bodies? Or did they disintegrate like the toad?

I nervously take a seat next to the fire. "Is there someplace I can go to get water and freshen up a bit, and maybe an outhouse?"

"There is a small pond a little off to the west. You can freshen up there and you will have to find a bush for your other needs. I won't follow you but I can hear you and your thoughts, and if you even think about trying to get away then this will be your last day alive." His voice is dead serious.

I cautiously stand. "See you in a couple." My lips spread to a cheesy grin.

The brush is thick but luckily the pond is very close. I splash the cool water on my face. How did I get myself in this mess? When I first arrived here, things came so easily—friends, my powers, allies—but lately I can't catch a break. First the spider bite, now this. I clean my hands and wash my face once more before departing back to the tree.

"Breakfast is ready." Saru shoves a large leaf with scrambled eggs on it up to my face.

I take the floppy plate, trying not to let it spill. Six months ago, I would never have imagined that I would eat eggs from an unknown species of bird, given to me on a leaf, and cooked by a monkey.

I eat the dripping eggs with my hands, trying to be proper, but Saru simply pours the scrambled mess from the pan into his mouth. "That was delicious. I usually have fish and rice for breakfast. It's been a long time since I've had scrambled eggs." I do my best to continue the cheery charade.

"Hmm, I'm glad I could please you," he says sarcastically. "Now, get back up the tree and give me peace and quiet while we wait for our next guest."

I dump the remaining food in my mouth and attempt to climb the tree, but it's too big for me to make much headway. When I fell I tore a patch of vines away, making this much harder.

Saru lets out a long winded sigh and grabs me around the waist. He carries me up one handed. "Thank you."

I try to clear my head of any thoughts, not wanting to agitate him. I'm so tired. I return to the middle of the platform where I spent the night. The floor is as hard as I remember, but before long exhaustion kicks in.

On occasion I'm awakened when there's a scuffle. At first, I was startled by the commotion, but with each yokai Saru defeats, I notice them less and less.

I fall asleep again and I dream about Hiroshi, coming back from his journey in the nick of time to save me. His firm arms carry me home, and as he bends his head down to kiss me, loud yelling yanks me awake.

"You thought you could lure me into a trap!" Someone violently growls. There is laughing and shouting by another voice as well, but neither is Saru. "Get the princess!" The first voice commands. I leap to my feet and a panther demon scales the tree up to the platform. She extends her claws.

"You're coming with us, princess." She slinks forward.

"No, I'm not." I attempt to activate my powers, but the light won't come. The panther demon rushes me and grabs my arms. "Get away!" I yell, kicking her knee.

"Ow!" Surprised by my attack she lets go long enough for me to get away. I scurry down the tree, slipping on the vines and jumping the last ten feet. I tumble to the ground shaking, she's close behind. I need to activate my powers to have any chance!

I take a deep breath and call upon the spirit energy of my ancestors. Mom, dad, please give me your strength. A sizzling sensation reverberates through me. At last my hands are aglow. *Thank God, thank the ancestors, thank somebody!*

Quickly, I create an energy whip and strike the panther. She cowers backward. I strike her again, knocking her to her kneels. I can easily end her life now, and I would take her life force.

Can I handle it? The intoxicating frenzy could overtake me. I raise my hand to strike her, I sense the itch to consume her soul. I force myself to use the energy whip to tie her hands and feet instead.

Saru is in battle with a male panther. He's much bigger than Saru; he's even taller than Hiroshi. The panther yokai slices his razor sharp claws against Saru's chest, ripping his tattered orange shirt. Blood stains his clothes as he grips his chest.

I could run away, but once they kill Saru, it won't be long before they track me down. I race toward the fight. I'll throw my lot in with the monkey over the panther.

"Ah, the princess wants to watch the show," the panther mocks. "Wait, what have you done with my companion?"

"She's busy right now," I sneer. Saru's eyes widen in horror. Before I realize what's transpiring, I'm pinned to the ground by the panther. His knees dig into my arms and pin them to my side. I struggle to sit up, he's too strong.

The lingering effect of the spider poison is still taking its toll on my ragged body. I activate the red light, but there's not much I can do with it.

He lifts his paw and extends his claws. I shut my eyes tight and await my fate, but death doesn't come. Opening my eyes, I see Saru holding the panther's elbow. I quickly wiggle my right arm free. The panther yokai swings his other paw hard against Saru.

I scream as he is thrown several feet away. A sickening crack courses through the air as he crashes to the ground.

I strain my neck to see him, but a thick plume of dust clouds my view. Was he trying to save me for himself, or because he changed his mind about me?

A half-growl half-laugh escapes the throat of the heavy yokai on top of me. I shoot my hand up to strike, but before I do, he's thrown off of me. I take a deep breath, my ribs able to expand without hesitation. What happened? Saru? No, it couldn't be.

I stand up to see Jiro strike the panther in the gut. His movement is swift and powerful, his fist indents the panther's stomach with the blow. Dazed the panther stumbles backwards.

Jiro kicks his ribs, breaking them with a debilitating crunch. The panther gasps for air, flailing his claws at Jiro. One of his strikes scrapes Jiro's arm, but he's unfazed. Jiro performs an uppercut to the panthers jaw and sends his head backwards, it snaps and the panther collapses dead.

Once that threat is subdued I run to Saru. He's face down on the ground motionless. I kneel beside him and roll him over. He turns his head to me. "I'm so sorry I brought you into this mess. I shouldn't have been so selfish. Now I will die from my foolish actions."

"Don't talk like that. You'll be fine." I wipe the blood trickling from a gash on his forehead.

"Please forgive me." He coughs, struggling to breathe.

"There's nothing that needs forgiving my friend." Saru smiles up at me and closes his eyes. He sucks in one more haggard breath and is gone.

"Rika? Rika?" Someone calls out to me.

216

"Miki?" I turn around to see Miki emerging from the woods.

"You're all right!" She rushes to hug me. "We got worried when you weren't at the river. What happened?"

"It's a long story, I'll tell you later. In the meantime, we need to do something with this panther and bury the bodies."

"I will take care of everything." Jiro steps in front of me.

Of course, he's the one to save the damsel in distress, again. "Thank you for coming. How did you find me?"

Jiro answers. "I came to visit you, and Miki told me you were missing. There's been a lot of yokai activity in the forest of Shinrin, and I've heard some disturbing rumors about kidnappings up here."

We're in the forest of Shinrin! Hiroshi and Okami are supposed to be here. Did they come, did Saru kill them? If they stumble upon us now they're sure to guess who I am.

We bury Saru near the tree we stayed in. My heart goes out to this poor man. He never had a real shot at a good life. The panther shouts vile curses at the villagers Jiro brought to decide the yokia's fate. After the villagers interrogate him, they find no other choice but execution.

Miki and I depart before punishment is carried out, with Jiro following close behind for protection. I gave him strict orders to return to Aimi once we were in the safety of the village, luckily he obliged.

Arriving home, we step through the doorway, and my jaw drops. Hiroshi and Okami? They're home! "What are you guys doing here?"

"You're not happy to see me?" Hiroshi kids.

"That's not what I meant." I hug Hiroshi. I'm glad he's safe.

"We barely got into the forest of Shinrin when we were attacked by monks. A group of holier than thou bald men who are bent on destroying the yokai to protect the princess."

Okami rubs his neck and pops it several times to the left. "They held us captive all night!"

"Crazy lunatics, there were fifty of them at least."

"I'd say more like a hundred!" Okami butts in.

"Whatever the number we didn't want to hurt them. They used a smoke bomb to disorient us, and their staff wielding skills were incredible."

"How did you get away?" Miki asks wide eyed.

"The monks weren't infallible and they got pretty drunk. Late this morning we were able to loosen the ropes binding us and sneak home."

"Will you go back?" I ask.

"No. While we were captive the monks had theory after theory on the princess's whereabouts. No one really knows where she is. No point running around the countryside with no end in sight."

I've dodged a bullet on this one, I can't let my guard down anymore. I have to stay on edge, if I don't I may not be so lucky next time.

19

"Are you awake yet?" A soft voice whispers in my ear, tickling them. It's still dark out, though there is enough light to see Hiroshi hovering over my bed.

What could he want at this hour? Rubbing my eyes and yawning, I reply, "Yes."

"I'm sorry to bother you, I thought we could watch the sun rise."

His eyes are wide awake with excitement. I shove the covers off, not wanting to disappoint him. "It sounds great, I need a few minutes to get ready." A grin spreads across his face, just the answer he was hoping for.

I dress and brush my hair. When it comes to placing my hair in the red comb he purchased for me, my tired brain and weak arms can't secure it. Time after time my hair unravels. I stretch my hair taut, and try again, ow! My hair snags in the teeth. Grr, my frustration builds.

"Do you need anything?" He asks from the other side of the dressing screen.

"I can't put my hair up." I try to be polite, yet my agitation is clear.

He folds the screen closed and gently takes the comb from my hand. "Save it for another time. You're beautiful no matter what." He sets it on the table, and we leave the hut hand in hand.

"Where exactly are we going?"

"You'll see." He squeezes my hand. "I've wanted to take you to this place since you arrived, but you always sleep in. When you were bitten by that spider, I decided if I was ever going to get the chance, I'd have to wake you up early. I'm sorry if you're tired, but it'll be worth it."

"Just a little groggy. I think that it is very sweet of you to go through all this trouble for me. I wish I could say I have something in store for you."

"Agreeing to come with me is enough." He always has the perfect romantic quip.

"Do you go here every morning?" We stray off the main path onto a less-traveled, windy dirt road up a steep hill.

"Usually, it's a place where I can clear my head, prepare myself for the day, and sort out my problems. It's become very special to me, the only person I've taken with me is Miki, although she's only come a few times because she doesn't enjoy the brisk morning air as I do. She'd rather sleep. I'm glad you are willing to make the journey. We've grown so close..." his voice trails off.

What was he going to say? I look to him for an answer, but he averts his eyes. "You're not going to leave it at that are you?"

"It's as if I've known you for years, not weeks. Please don't find that creepy."

"Why would I? It's not like you're stalking me. We do live together, it's not that hard to believe you would know me pretty well by now."

We reach the top of the hill, and Hiroshi takes a seat upon a fallen tree. "Rika, it's not only getting to know you, it's a familiarity about how I feel about you."

I sit next to him, the dry rot on the log causes it to be softer than I had anticipated. "And how *do* you feel about me?"

He hesitates, contemplating whether to proceed. I scooch closer and bump my sandal against his bag. "I bet you're starving." He prattles on to the next subject. "Miki always is by this point. Here, I bought these sticky buns last night."

My mouth waters as he removes the sugar coated balls of doughy goodness from a bamboo food box inside his pack. I haven't had sweets since I left Earth. "They're amazing."

He hands me two buns. I inhale and smell their sweet cinnamon scent, then I gaze at them and imagine how glorious they will taste, and then finally eat them one tiny bite at a time.

I savor the sweet flavor as long as possible, holding the sugar on my tongue, and all too soon both of my buns are gone. "Those were incredible. Thank you."

"It was nothing."

A gust of wind blows up the hill and washes over me, causing me to shiver.

"Oh, how stupid of me." Hiroshi lightly bumps his forehead with his palm. "You must be freezing. I can't believe I didn't think to bring a blanket. It's coldest right before sun up." He wraps his arm around me and tucks me in close. "I suppose I will keep you warm."

Did he plan this? I don't know, and I don't really care. It feels nice to be held in his arms. No boy on Earth ever held me like this. I lean my head on his bare chest, although the air is nippy, his skin is warm to the touch. Smoothly with his other arm, he takes my other hand in his and coils his fingers around mine.

The orange burst of light breaks through the horizon as the sun begins its journey upward. The morning hike we took didn't feel very long, but it must have taken us awhile to get to this height.

Perhaps it's because of Hiroshi, I lose track of time when I'm with him. From this view we can look over the entire village, and even part of the cherry orchard. "I've never seen anything so beautiful."

"I have," Hiroshi speaks in a low voice. Turning my head up, I lock onto the morning light sparkling in his flecks of silver in his eyes. "The sunrise from this hill was once the most amazing sight I had ever seen, until I met you."

"Hiroshi, I…"

Before another word passes my lips, he leans down and kisses me. I promptly close my eyes and receive his kiss with grace, even though on the inside I'm freaking out.

He lightly lifts his lips from mine, this time it's not rushed. He caresses my cheek with his callused hand. "I love you. I fell in love with you the moment I caught you in my arms the day we met. I told you once before while you were sick, but it's no surprise you don't remember."

"To tell you the truth, I heard you telling me before. It's why I kept fighting to live. I was too nervous to say anything afterwards." I gulp, getting up the nerve I say, "I love you too." After a long pause I ask, "Um, now what?"

"I suppose we do what most people do, get married. I'm pretty sure that's how the cycle goes." He winks.

Wow, things are short here in Nihon; back on Earth people date for years before getting engaged. I guess people don't have the time for long courtships here, what with the demon attacks and all.

My mind is swept up in the fairytale romance, he basically admitted he wants to marry me. The thought of marriage brings a singe of iciness through my body. What am I talking about? It's not like I'm allowed to marry him anyway.

What does it matter if he thinks we should get married in two weeks or two years? No matter the case, Aimi will not tolerate it, I'm the princess, not some common girl.

"Since I'm yokai, I had little chance of falling in love. You've changed all of that." Hiroshi kisses my forehead.

"Why didn't you ever date a yokai like yourself?"

"I've thought about it, but most aren't like me. They are rude, blood-thirsty monsters. I don't want to spend the rest of my life with anyone like that. I want a companion, a friend."

"I see what you mean."

His eyes become stern and he clears his throat. "Rika, this is forward of me, but why should we wait any longer? Marry me."

My breath catches. My heart skips a beat and then another. He's proposing! He's really proposing. Am I ready for this? I haven't even graduated from high school. My mind races, 'till I remember Jiro, again.

I can't commit to him while I'm technically promised to another man. "I need time to think about it."

The corners of his eyes droop in disappointment. "I understand."

"I love you Hiroshi, I will give you an answer soon, I promise."

He half smiles. I can't stand to see him like this. I slip my hands around his shoulders and kiss him with more passion than I ever thought I could feel about a man. He places his hand on the small of my back. If only I could be his, to run away with him and never think of politics or arranged marriages ever again.

He escorts me home, as any gentlemen would. I squeeze his hand, how much longer will I be able to stay with him? I grip his hand tighter, I wish I never had to let go.

20

Drumming my fingers on the solid table, I try to sort out my options. Yesterday Hiroshi proposed! But I'm technically engaged to Jiro. And Hiroshi is still hunting the princess, which is me!

Still in my night shirt, I push the pile of cold rice around in the wooden bowl. What to do, what to do?! Hiroshi has been extra sweet these past 24 hours, how can a refuse? But how can I accept?

Lost in the trance of my conundrum, I hear shouts outside. "Hiroshi, come quick!" It sounds like Haru, though I'm not sure.

I throw on my kimono and run outside whilst tying the obi. The warning bell rings loudly, as it does each time the village is under attack. Squawks and screams emanate over the clanging of the bell. A distinct scream pierces through the chaos, Miki!

226

I force my legs to move faster. I round a corner to find Hiroshi in combat with one of the crow demons. That's the one who attacked me when I first arrived. He's back.

I activate my powers and sneak up from behind, lifting my fist to punch the crow. He spins around. "Not this time." He catches my wrist. "You didn't think you could get away with that, did you?"

The crow spreads his wings and prepares to take flight. He flaps his massive wings and grabs my other hand. "Since we keep running into each other, I might as well introduce myself. I'm Kagemaru, leader of this murder of crows." With a swift movement of his neck he slams his head into mine, knocking me out.

I regain consciousness to the sound of screaming. Hiroshi claws into Kagemaru's back. Hiroshi swings again and slashes part of his wing. Kagemaru grips my wrists even tighter, refusing to relinquish me and we sail higher. Hiroshi strikes the demon's other wing.

His wing crumples up, and he whispers in my ear, "You'll regret resisting me." We sink back toward the ground and he drops me.

With a screech from Kagemaru, other crows pick up villagers and fly off with them. "We've got to stop them!" Hiroshi leaps into the air, grabbing villagers one by one out of the crows' claws.

Just ahead, three villagers are being carried away. I chase after them, thrusting volleys of daggers up, being careful not to hit the villagers. Hiroshi follows me and catches the villagers as they drop. My legs are tired, and I'm struggling to keep up with the last crow. Just one more.

I throw wave of light daggers. The demon swoops to the left, dodging them. Before I can attempt another attack, the yokai clutches the villager's neck with its claws and wrenches hard. His body goes limp and his once kicking legs dangle lifelessly, he's dead.

"*No no no!* You can't do that!" I scream. My feet slow down, I've failed them. In an instant, a fire kindles within me and I take off at full speed.

"Aahhh! Die already!" I throw light daggers over and over in a blurry rage, until the demon crumbles to pieces in midflight.

My heavy legs overwhelm me, sending me to my knees. Trembling I shout out all my frustration. "Why did you have to do it? I could have saved him." I choke back tears, barely able to catch my breath. "I should have been faster."

A crawling sensation spreads from my chest to the tips of my fingers. The desire to kill more yokai is on the brink of explosion. My wild eyes search for a release, but Hiroshi is the only yokai in sight. I shun away from him.

Hiroshi grabs my arm and twirls me around to face him. "It's not your fault. These things happen. You have killed the demon, it's done."

I squeeze my eyes shut, I have no idea if my eyes will change color. It would be a dead giveaway. I shake my head, trying to clear it.

He shakes me slightly, "Snap out of it."

My balled fists relax, the overwhelming emotions trickle away. When I ended the frog demons life, the call to use my powers came, this time it came again but mixed with rage.

Something inside me has changed, and it happens each time I kill. The frenzy that takes over is frightening. What if I use my powers on Hiroshi? What if I can't control myself next time? I don't want to feel this way ever again.

"Rika, have you seen Miki?" Hiroshi asks impatiently, as if for the second time.

I swing back into reality. "Miki. Where is she? I thought I heard her in trouble." A new panic sets in.

"We've got to find her. Hop on my back." I climb on, and we take off. I'm getting better at adjusting my kimono with only a moment's notice.

"Did you kill Kagemaru?" I ask.

"No, he's injured, but he'll live." Hiroshi answers.

My heart sinks to the pit of my stomach, things have been too easy with him, it's like he's testing us. There's no way he'll be gone for long, he's planning something.

And to make matters worse it's not just me who's in danger, by me staying here all the people of Unmei are sucked into this. The man who died was because of me. Guilt courses through my body.

"We need to find Miki. The scent of her blood is in the air. I'll carry you." His voice has an icy edge to it.

People pop out of their homes as we pass by. "Thank you for saving us," they call out. With each minute they become more complacent, but my reaction is the opposite.

Moments later, there she is, lying there on the ground in a pool of blood. Oh no, my heart sinks even lower.

"Miki, Miki, wake up!" Hiroshi cries out. I slide off his back as he kneels down next to her motionless body. "I must take her to Igaku. That is her only chance for survival."

Poor Miki. This is all my fault. It should be me down there, not her. About to wallow in regret, I'm snapped out of it by an agonizing moan. I scan the area and see Okami lying unconscious only a few yards away. "Okami's injured as well."

Hiroshi quickly examines him. "He's hurt, but he will pull through. Stay here with Okami. I need to take Miki to Igaku immediately."

Returning to Miki, he gently lifts her into his arms. Turning now to me, he says, "I love you Rika. Be safe, and take care of Okami and the villagers while I'm gone. I will return in a few days." He kisses me and sprints into the forest.

"I love you too." A tear rolls down my cheek. "Be safe," I whisper, even though I know he can't hear me. I fall to my knees and tend to my first patient.

Blood pulsates from wounds in both his arms near his shoulders. I press my hands against the gashes, "Okami, Okami, wake up."

"Ume, is that you?" He mutters. "Ume, I've missed you so much. How are you here with me? I knew you'd come back to me."

"It's me, Rika."

Realization comes to him. "Of course it's you. Who else would it be?" His voice has returned to its normally abrasive tone. "I'll manage. Go help the villagers. I can make it home on my own." He swats me away and stands up. Within a split second his face flashes to a pale white and he keels over.

"Stubborn fool, you need me to get home." I lift my arm under his and pull him up.

"Fine," he reluctantly agrees. He slumps against my shoulder, practically bending at the waist, and I assist him back home.

"Miyu, I need your help," I call out to her as soon as we step through the doorway.

"Oh my." She stands there, stunned. Blood droplets splatter on the floor.

"I need wet rags and clean bandages." She remains paralyzed, staring at crimson red pooling on the ground, "Miyu!" I shout.

She snaps to attention. "Yes. Right away." She rushes to one of the shelves and retrieves the supplies.

I lay Okami down and try to comfort him. "You'll be fixed up in no time. Once you're cleaned up and bandaged you can sleep in a nice comfy bedroll."

Miyu attempts to hand me the wet rags and bandages. "Here they are, just as you asked."

"I need you to tend to him while I take care of the villagers. I'm not sure if there are more wounded."

"I'm unsure if I can do this, the sight of blood has always been an issue for me." Her face pales.

231

"You have to. Miyu, you can do this. This is where I'll bring any injured. I'm counting on you." She places the supplies in her lap and nods absently. "I will be back soon."

Outside, the scene before me is grim. Several huts are on fire, others are smashed to pieces, while a few are damaged but remain intact. Those yokai have really torn this place apart with record speed. We came as fast as we could. Perhaps they're trying to send me a message.

"Rika!" Jiro runs to me.

Impeccable timing, I knew he couldn't stay away long. "I'm fine." Before he can kiss me I wrap my arms around him.

"For heaven's sake Sarah," he whispers in my ear and strokes my hair. "You're not safe here."

"I'm not safe anywhere. Now, I need you to search for those who are injured and bring them to my house."

He gives me a stern look. "I will do my best, but when this is over, we need to talk."

"Fine, I'll meet up with you later." I drop my arms to leave.

"Until then." He kisses my hand before briskly walking away.

My work is nonstop for hours, searching for survivors and burying the dead. I was upset when one villager died. I had no idea there was more, fourteen to be exact. The horror of this ordeal will be forever seared in my memory. I should leave before anyone else dies.

It's well passed my bedtime when I finally return home. Jiro is waiting for me inside. "Rika." He rises to greet me.

"I'm finished for today." I plop myself next to the table.

"I have searched through the village twice to ensure no one else needs us. All of the villagers who have been brought here will recover. Miyu has been taking great care of them."

"Thank you. I would still be out there if you hadn't come along to help me." I rest my forehead on the hardwood table.

Why does he have to make things so easy and difficult, all at the same time? He's the perfect gentlemen and so helpful. If Hiroshi and I hadn't connected, there's a chance I would be madly in love with Jiro.

"No need to thank me. Now, you must be famished. Miyu made soup for everyone about an hour ago. I know we have leftovers." He walks to the cupboard and pulls out a bowl and spoon.

"Thank you."

"Would you like me to heat it up for you?"

"No. I'm too hungry."

"I thought you'd say that." The bowl clatters on the table, causing the soup to slosh. "Sorry."

"Don't worry about it." I slurp up the thin broth.

"Miyu invited me to stay the night to help her take care of the wounded. You don't mind, do you?"

"Why would I?" I dip the empty bowl and spoon into a bucket of water and place them in the washing basin.

"It's no secret me being here makes you uneasy I've been told tales of the lion protector and his girlfriend, soon to be juji."

"Where not juji, yet." I lift my chin and square my shoulders. I glance around the room, not everyone is asleep yet. Okami's wide awake in my bedroll, starring up at the ceiling blankly.

Jiro takes note but still steps close to me. I back away and bump into the counter. "Congratulations on your soon to be engagement."

His words say one thing, but the look in his eyes say something very different. If we were alone, he'd probably berate me for being so foolish, and maybe he's right, but it still doesn't change the way I feel.

Okami lets out a soft groan.

"Duty calls. Good night." I slip away to Okami, I could almost hug him for saving me from that awkward situation. "How are you doing?"

"I'm fine." His voice is stern at first, but then it softens, "Thank you Rika."

"You are welcome. And since I did save your life and all, can I ask you a question?"

He rolls his eyes, "Just one."

"Who is Ume?"

"A girl." He rolls over.

"That was pitiful. Rescuing you is worth more than that."

"Fine, if you must know, Ume was my wife."

"What happened to her? Why isn't she with you?"

"Those are more questions. You'll have to save my life a few more times if you want me to answer those."

"Come on, it's all part of the same question, sort of. Please."

"If it will shut you up, then fine. If you tell anyone though, you'll be the one that needs saving." His eyes glare at me.

"I promise, I won't tell anyone." I cross my heart with my fingers.

"Ume was the loveliest human, much prettier than you. She was smart, sweet—" He clears his throat, "We were only married two years when our village was under siege by yokai. I was in town getting her a present when they attacked.

"I tried to find her, but she wasn't at home. I searched for her everywhere. She had gone out looking for me. When I finally found her, they killed her, right in front of me. I slaughtered those demons, every last one of them. I won't stop until I'm the most powerful thing on this planet."

"I'm so sorry."

"I don't need your pity. I don't care anymore. Humans are weak and pathetic. I should have seen that before I married one." No wonder he's so cold. He hardened his heart long ago to keep it safe.

"Good night." I leave his side to find a free space on the floor to curl up and sleep.

The next morning, I awake to people moaning in pain. I get off the floor and stretch my sore back. It's going to be a long day.

"Good morning sunshine." Okami throws a pillow at me.

"Hey, what was that for?"

"For sleeping in." He snatches the pillow from the man next to him and throws it at me.

"Cut that out." I laugh, trying to block it.

"I'm hungry and I've been waiting for you to wake up for hours. Hurry or I'll grab another." His hand hovers over a woman's tan pillow.

"Fine, fine, I'm going." I hop over several people on the floor to get to the food pantry. "Where's Miyu and Jiro?"

"She's out gathering herbs, and he's in town getting more medical supplies. You get the privilege of chef."

I retrieve leftover rice balls and bring them to Okami.

He scrunches his nose, giving me a sour face. "How do you expect me to eat these?"

"With your hands and your mouth."

"It's cold. Can't you heat it up?" He whines.

"I thought you were a tough demon that didn't need a bedroll and could go for days without sleep."

236

"Fine, if you can't heat it up, I will eat it cold because I am a big tough demon."

"Here you go." I chuckle and hand him the bowl.

"Thanks." He smiles taking the food. He smiled. He actually smiled.

"So you *can* smile, I was beginning to think it was my imagination."

"Don't tell anyone." He squints his eyes, and I crack up.

I serve the others breakfast. The rest of the day goes by smoothly. I labor with the villagers to rebuild their homes and assist Miyu in caring for the injured. Jiro remains on the sidelines, helping out where he can. He keeps his distance from me, probably upset that I've rejected him.

Me rejecting a guy, my previous dream guy, that's a new one. I can't refrain from feeling remorse about everything. He's always been nice to me, and it is my obligation to marry him. I'm so confused. Everything will be sorted out once Hiroshi is back; at least I hope it will.

21

Six days have passed since the crows attacked with no word from Hiroshi. Miki's injuries must be worse than expected. Miyu and I have been so busy that this last week has been a blur. Counting the days becomes harder and harder, at times I lose track altogether. I honestly don't know how long I've been on Nihon.

With all the wounded villagers back to their homes and most of the town repaired, now is the perfect opportunity to visit with Aimi. I can explain things and try to reason with her about me marrying Hiroshi.

"Good morning," Miyu chirps. "You are up early today. Breakfast is still warm. Did you not sleep well?"

"I'm energized, ready to conquer the day."

"I see, can't take your mind off of Hiroshi." Miyu giggles. "I'd have trouble sleeping too if I were you."

"It's true, I haven't rested well since he left with Miki. I pray she's ok."

"Me too, ancestors willing, she'll pull through." She wipes her hands on her apron and with a lighter tone she says, "I'm tired of you moping around all the time. Don't dwell on the things you can't change."

"Yes Miyu." I scarf down my breakfast and hurry out the door. I briskly walk along the path, almost jogging to the cherry orchard.

"Rika," I hear a voice call out. I turn to see Jiro waving to me. I stop and allow him to catch up. "Where are you headed this morning? I thought you'd still be worn out from all the long hours you've put in."

"Is it a crime to take a stroll? Besides, you're awake and it's barely past sun up."

"Point taken. Do you mind if I join you?"

"Sure, why not?" He offers me his arm to escort. I hesitantly accept. The sleeve of his cotton kimono is surprisingly soft, he's sporting a grayish green colored one today.

"Is there anywhere in particular you're heading?"

"The cherry orchard, to see Aimi."

His voice sparks an interest, "Are you having second thoughts about marrying Hiroshi?"

I shake my head. "That's not it. Quite the opposite in fact."

People wave to us as they pass by, we smile and return the gesture. Once we are out of ear shot Jiro speaks to me in a hushed tone, "I know you have your heart set on marriage with a yokai, going to Aimi is a mistake. She will not accept this."

He doesn't face me as he talks, not wanting to arouse suspicion I guess. As we stray further from town there are fewer villagers, but we continue the indirect conversation anyway.

"I still have to try."

"Why? Am I really such a bad guy that you are forced into the arms of a demon? A man out for your life." The last sentence is hardly audible it's so quiet.

"It's not that. It's not that at all." I don't even know what to say at this point. I'm being selfish, putting my own desires above the welfare of an entire world. I need to change the subject, but what am I supposed to do, talk about the weather? We step off the path and enter the cherry orchard.

The petals rain down throughout the orchard. Piles of flowers lie along the ground. The orchard must be under an enchantment to continually flow with this many petals.

In an instant, Jiro glides his body in front of mine and slides his fingers through my hair. "Please Sarah, we could be happy together. He'll move on, there are plenty of women who adore him, but you and me, we're meant to be."

My heart leaps, "Brandon, you don't understand. I don't love you anymore." The words burn as they leave my tongue.

I can see the pain in his eyes. The soft pink petals fall on his black hair. "I still love you, and I always will."

He pulls me closer and he kisses me, his lips linger upon mine.

I don't mind his kiss, it's closure, a farewell to each other. He lifts his head, without looking at me he holds out his bent elbow, and I clasp my hands around it. "I will take you to Aimi now."

In silence, he escorts me through the maze of trees. The curtains of flowers hampers my sense of direction, it will be difficult to find my way back without him. He's a good friend, I'll give him that.

Before long, a gray haired woman comes into view. "Aimi?" I call out.

"Rika, is that you?"

I race forward and she holds out her arms welcoming me. "It so good to see you," I say as we hug briefly. "Did you give my mother the letter?"

"Yes, I did. I'm not sure if she read it, but I put it on your bed back on Earth."

"Thank you so much."

Jiro cuts in. "I will leave the two of you to chat. Rika, I will meet up with you later." He kisses my hand and departs.

"So much has happened since we last saw each other. You're skills have improved so much that stories are starting to spread about you and Hiroshi." She gives me a sly look.

"I hope all good."

She smiles, her old voice full of charm. "Of course, I would expect nothing less from the princess. People are marveling that a human and yokai have teamed together for the sake of helping others. I guess it was a good decision for you to stay with that lion yokai after all. He has taught you a lot. I'm very proud of you."

"Well, thank you. I have been practicing hard. I want to become the person this world needs."

Aimi sighs, "You are ready Rika, you have to leave your friends and take your rightful place. You understand that, don't you?"

My breath catches in my throat. "I have news about Hiroshi and me."

"What?"

"He's proposed."

"What? When did this happen?"

"Only recently. It's not something I planned on. Please don't be mad. I haven't given him an answer."

"Now this really complicates things." Aimi pauses, rubbing her chin. "Have you told him about your true identity?"

"No, he has no idea."

"Then we can still salvage the situation."

"What do you mean?" I ask.

"Nothing, only that this matter needs to be dealt with very carefully to ensure your safety. I will come up with a plan on how to break the news to him. I will send

Jiro with instructions for you. In the meantime, get your affairs in order and be prepared to leave for the castle at a moment's notice. Before your identity is out it will be imperative you seek shelter there."

"Isn't the castle a little obvious?"

"Yes, but we are organizing an army from Maaku to meet with us at the castle. It is a great location to defend attacks, it will show authority to your subjects. Trust me on this."

I nod, "Yes Aimi."

"Good, I will send you word when we are ready. Good bye Rika." She hugs me one last time before vanishing between the trees.

How will Hiroshi react when I tell him? When and how should I reveal the truth? Maybe I should plan some sort of date and tell him then. No, I shouldn't make it out to be such a big deal, but it is a big deal. I should—

"What are you so deep in thought about?" I'm startled by Okami's voice. I whip around almost bumping into him. How long has he been here? I take a step back, trying to compose myself. "Since Hiroshi proposed, I've been contemplating my answer."

"Hmm, you could have been deciding your wedding, but somehow I bet you were thinking about something else."

Oh no, he heard. My palms start to sweat.

"I can see by the dumbfounded look on your face that you've realized my suspicions have been confirmed. Don't be too surprised. I'm not an idiot. Talking so openly about a secret that big, tsk tsk. You're the princess."

243

He takes a long stride toward me. "I've been scouring Nihon for a long time and I've finally found her. The best part is I know her. I know her powers, how she fights, how she thinks. Killing her will be easier than I dreamed. Don't you think?"

He raises his arm to strike me. He swings, but I duck and run away into the trees. "You can run, but I'm faster."

He's right. He's a wolf yokai. I don't get very far before he pounces on top of me, pinning me to the ground. "Any last words, Princess? Any royal decree or declaration you'd like to make?" He lifts his arm ready to claw his way through me.

What should I do? I try to wiggle free, but his knees drive into my sides. Then, before I can make another move, Jiro tackles him from the side, knocking him off me. Okami thrusts Jiro away and scrambles to his feet. "Don't get in my way!" he growls. Jiro hits the ground hard and lies unconscious.

I ascend to my feet and activate my powers. Okami charges and I throw energy daggers at him. He dodges them easily and continues toward me.

"You didn't think you could get me with that trick, did you?" I create an energy whip and slap Okami across the face. "Just give up. You're only prolonging the inevitable."

My attack only slows him down, but it gives Jiro the time to regain consciousness and tackle him again.

"Now you're really starting to get on my nerves." Okami rips Jiro off him and tosses him aside.

With Okami distracted, I use the energy whip like a rope and begin binding his hands. I've tied one hand, though I can't grab the other one. With one hard yank of his arm he's free. "Now it's time for you to die."

"Not yet!" Jiro yells as he jumps onto Okami and shoves a cloth into his face. Within seconds, Okami becomes limp and falls to the ground.

"Jiro, I can't believe you've stopped him. What is that?"

"It's a special herb that will make anyone unconscious, even yokai, but the effect doesn't last long. Let's go." He grabs my hand and we dart through the orchard. I don't know what I would have done if Jiro hadn't been there.

I've got to reach the castle. Osamu is there, the army will be arriving. It's my best chance, but Okami's too strong, too fast, how will I ever make it in time? The castle is days away. Hiroshi, he can get me there, and he's only a few hours from Unmei. If I can make it to him I'll be alright.

My secret's out. I manage to find my way through the orchard and race through town with Jiro in tow. People stare at me and complain as I push past them. I'm being rude but I can't slow down. I must get to Hiroshi.

The village gates are up ahead, I'm nearly out of town. Now through the forest and on to Igaku. Still no sign of Okami, it's a relief but he'll be after me soon. I should have tied him up.

As I pass through the wooden gates, Okami's voice booms through the air. "I'll find you Rika! You think you can escape me, but I will kill you if it's the last thing I do!"

22

He's after me. I must run faster.

"I'll try to slow him down." Jiro flashes a daring smile before turning back.

I sprint through the forest, breathing hard, running as fast as my legs will carry me. My lungs are going to burst. I'm running too fast and I don't jump high enough to clear the log lying in the road. I land on the hard rocky path, partially knocking me out.

"You think you can run away from me, Princess? You can't hide you're true nature from me. You can't run, you can't hide. I will find you!" Okami cries out from close behind.

I stumble to my feet and continue. Branches snap and twigs break in the forest beside me. I have to follow the path, but Okami can run through the woods as a shortcut. Hiroshi said that it was only a few hours away. I've been running for about an hour now. My body is slowing down, while Okami is ever growing closer.

I force myself to keep going, but it's not enough. Okami breaks through the trees and tackles me to the ground. "I've got you now Princess."

No you don't. I activate my powers and rip his hands off me.

"Aah!" he yells in pain. I turn to run, quickly he chases after me. "Come back here!" He grabs my arm and pulls me close.

"No!" With the red energy light in my hands, I tear his hand away from my arm and punch him several times. Okami is stunned at the initial blow, but shakes it off and clutches my throat and lifts me off my feet.

"Your soul is mine." He squeezes harder and harder, a vein in his bicep bulges out from the pressure.

I lift my hand and throw energy daggers at his chest.

He releases me to clutch his chest. "You'll pay for that. I was going to make your death quick and painless, but now I will enjoy taking my time."

Before he can make good on his threat, I use my powers to create an energy whip to strike him down to the ground.

I strike again and again until his body lies limp, now's my chance to finish him off. I stand with my right arm hovering over him, hand glowing, ready to unleash the final attack. I hesitate. If I kill him, the change will happen again.

Will I be able to control it? The impending hysteria jolts me away, scared of who I might become if I allow myself to follow through. I tie up him with an energy rope and leave him lying there.

I travel quickly for several more hours, worrying the entire time if Okami will catch up with me. I haven't heard him. Please God, let my energy rope hold. Finally, Igaku comes into view. Thank goodness. Now, to find Hiroshi and Miki.

I approach the first villager I see. Completely out of breath, I manage to get out my words. "Have you seen Hiroshi? He is a lion yokai. He brought in a little girl a few days ago. She was severely injured."

The villager bows his head and shakes it slowly. "That poor little thing, I heard she didn't make it. You could try looking for him at the clinic."

My breath ceases, it's as if I've been punched in the gut.

"Take this dirt road about one mile, then turn right at the fork in the road. That will take you to the center of town. You can't miss it."

"Thank you," I manage to choke out. I bow and race down the path. *He's wrong he must be wrong.*

I get to the split in the road and turn right. More and more huts come into view. I'm almost there, just a little farther. I push myself for the finishing stretch, but I crash into a cart full of cabbage and knock the entire load over.

"What have you done!" The middle aged man hauling the cart yells at me.

"I'm sorry." I turn to keep running.

An armored guard blocks my path. "What is your business here in Igaku?" he demands.

"I'm looking for a lion yokai named Hiroshi. He came here a few days ago with a little girl who was hurt. It's really important that I find him."

"You're too late. He's already left."

"What do you mean he's already left? I was told he's still here. I really need to find him."

"Why are you in such a hurry to find this demon?"

"I need his help. Please let me through."

"You are going to need to come with me." He takes hold of my arm.

"Why? This was an accident." I point to the mess of vegetables.

"I don't know where you're from, but here we take property damage seriously. I'm bringing you in to see if there are any warrants out for your arrest."

It's not the law I'm running from. "Sir, I really don't have time for this. I need to get to my friend." I struggle a little bit but let him take me to the center of the village for questioning. At least if I'm taken to the middle of the city, Hiroshi might be there.

We walk for several minutes, the guard dragging me along. It's nice to slow down after all that running except I must find Hiroshi as soon as possible. We come to a stop in front of a jailhouse. He yanks me inside and tosses me into one of the cells. "What are you doing? Let me out of here. I haven't done anything wrong."

"You can wait here for a while and cool off. Then I will ask you some questions, like why you're with a demon. Those scum are murderers, no doubt you are too." The guard locks the door and plops down in his chair.

"You don't understand. There is a yokai after me. If you don't let me out soon, he will come here, and he will stop at nothing to assassinate me."

"I'm sure you'd say just about anything to get out of the holding cell." He's not going to listen to me. Okami will be here soon. He's probably woken up by now and on his way. If I don't get out of here quickly, I'd hate to think about what would happen. I could activate my powers and throw energy daggers at the wooden bars. They'd probably break fairly easily.

While contemplating my escape, screams emanate from outside. Too late. "You stay here. I'll be back." The guard scurries out the door.

"No, wait!" I reach my arm through the bars of the holding cell door. "Come back."

There are more screams as people run past the jailhouse. Now's the time to use my escape plan. I engage my powers and step back from the door. I fling my arm out and toss streaks of light at the door until it breaks apart enough for me to press through.

Outside the jailhouse, I find several guards standing in front of Okami down the street. I have to help them, they have no idea what he's capable of. I rush toward them, my hands red with energy. "Get away from them Okami!" I order.

"I knew I'd find you here. Running to your boyfriend for help. It won't help you. He's already left.

You were too late. Besides, he wants you dead just as much as I do, maybe even more."

"You're lying. He wasn't on the trail."

"He probably took one of the shortcuts through the forest, like I did. Great minds think alike you know. He wanted to get back to you, how sweet. He's probably only now finding out that you're not there."

"Now who's the one lying?" I try to remain strong, but he's probably telling the truth. "I should have killed you when I had the chance."

"You were too weak and you are still are." He races toward me. I dodge him and try to punch him. "Not this time." Okami says, grabbing my arm and twisting it.

A guard sneaks up behind Okami, his sword lifted above his head to slash the yokai. Okami hears the guard and spins around, striking the man in the head with his free hand. With one blow, he slaughters the guard, but he shows no sign of remorse.

"You killed that man!"

His eyes flash red. "Doesn't matter. I've killed countless. Each time, my powers increase, making it easier to destroy you. It's been so hard resisting while I've been traveling with you and your band of do-gooders. There's such a thrill when you murder. You really ought to try it."

"I could never be like you."

"That's where you're wrong. You will have to kill to protect yourself and once you feel what it's like, there's no going back."

He grips tighter, his claws dig into my arm, causing it to bleed.

He's wrong. I have killed and I'm still the same. I have to save myself. He cuts into me deeper and a droplet of blood splatters on my foot. He inhales deeply and smiles.

An idea hits me, what if my feet can project my energy? Then I can fight back. I focus on my toes and summon the energy. Glancing down to my delight, my feet are surrounded by the red light. I kick Okami hard in the knee.

"Ahh! You little brat!" He loosens his claws for a split second, giving me the opening I need. I yank away and toss energy daggers at him. The first volley of energy daggers strikes him in the gut, but he evades the second wave.

"Give it up Okami!" I shout, unleashing a stream of daggers at him. He manages to dodge most of them.

He gathers up his strength and charges, ignoring the pain of my attacks and knocking me down to the ground. He kicks me hard in the side. He kneels down, pressing his claws around my throat. "Your life ends now."

A guard comes up from behind Okami and slams his sword onto Okami's shoulder. Okami frees his hand from my neck to hit the guard, giving me a chance to spring to my feet. Tossing several waves of energy daggers, I run, hoping to lose Okami in the trees.

My lungs burn, and my calves ache, they beg me to give up. I press the thought of defeat into a tiny box in my brain and shut the lid. In defiance of myself I pick up speed, if my body is going to complain, I'll give it something to complain about. I just have to keep moving.

Twigs snap in the forest beside me. Not again. Okami couldn't have caught up so quickly, could he? To my relief, it's not Okami who emerges from, but Hiroshi. I'm saved!

I stumble to a halt. Exasperated, I can hardly speak, "Hiroshi someone's after me. I need your help."

"Calm down. What happened?" He examines my bleeding arms. "Who did this to you?"

"Okami."

"Okami? Why would he do this?" He brushes away the hair stuck to the sweat on my face. I have to tell him I'm the princess. No matter what the price.

I take a deep breath. "Hiroshi, I've wanted to explain for a long time now, but it was never the right moment." Here goes nothing. "Hiroshi…I'm the princess.

Pronunciation Guide

Aimi (ah-ee-mee)	**Miyu** (mee-yoo)
Akari (ah-kah-ree)	**Mizumi** (mee-zoo-mee)
Haru (hah-roo)	**Nihon** (nee-ho-n)
Heiwa (heh-ee-wah)	**Okami** (oh-kah-mee)
Hiroshi (hee-ro-shee)	**Onnakono-nomi** (oh-nah-koh-noh-noh-mee)
Igaku (ee-gah-koo)	**Osamu** (oh-sah-moo)
Jiro (jee-roh)	**Rika** (ree-kah)
Juji (joo-jee)	**Ritsuko** (ree-t-su-koh)
Kagemaru (kah-geh-mah-roo)	**Saru** (sah-roo)
Katsuki (kah-t-su-ki)	**Shinrin** (shih-n-rih-n)
Kenta (keh-n-tah)	**Takara** (tah-kah-rah)
Maaku (mah-koo)	**Unmei** (oo-n-meh-ee)
Mirai (mee-rah-ee)	**Yokai** (yoh-kah-ee)
Miki (mee-kee)	

About the Author

Jennie Peters is a happy mother to two wonderful children. She loves homeschooling them and exploring their farm together. When she's not kicking it as a stay at home mom, she plays and teaches piano. This story has been a dream of hers since taking Japanese in middle school. Thanks for being a part of her dream come true!

Follow Jennie on Facebook
https://www.facebook.com/Jennie.Lynn.Peters

www.ingramcontent.com/pod-product-compliance
Lightning Source LLC
Chambersburg PA
CBHW020400210626
46816CB00006BB/2052